DIARY

OF

A DIVINE
RELATIONSHIP

Jack & Kelly

THERESA A. LAWS

Acknowledgments

Thank you to those who have helped in whatever way possible, be it reading, editing, critiquing, etc. or be it instilling in me the idea that there was indeed a book in me. The journey has not been easy, but most importantly thanks be to God who inspired this message, encouraged and supported me.

Our pain can lead to purpose.
It's where our character is most effectively shaped.

PROLOGUE

"**W**ELL, I SURE HOPE they do fix it real nice like a house I've been dreamin' about. I hope we don't have any problems getting it. It's 1976 in Jackson, MS. We both been through a lot in our young years but thank God our girls won't have to bear what we've been through. Things ain't perfect here but they're better, so I'm looking forward to a real home. My girls need space, a backyard, and I need a nice kitchen. We 'bout to have another one running 'round here so we need that house," Emma said to her husband as she caressed her bulge of a belly. She knew the baby was always listening.

"They're gonna have it," affirmed Charles. "I'm telling you, if it's the last thing I do." He reached for her hand and kissed it. "If it's the *last* thing I do!"

Emma raised her eyebrows at Charles. "Well, why you did ya have to say somethin' like that now? Geez! I didn't want to hear that! You're the healthiest fella I know. I have sho fed you good. I been holdin' back the salt as the doctor said and you been exercising. That blood pressure went down to normal with no medication. I know what you meant, but I don't like that kind of talk. Things are about to turn around for good with the baby and the new house. We've got to keep the faith."

Days later while Charles was at work, his wife was home and felt the all too familiar first pangs of labor. She asked her neighbor, Mr. Henderson, to drive her to the hospital but his brand new car was the only vehicle available. His son had borrowed his older model. Mr. Henderson seethed within himself and prayed for his car seats more than for the pregnant woman's ordeal. Emma tried to pay him no mind as she told him Charles would be so thankful and would return a much-needed favor one day. *My next-door neighbor is a crusty old soul, how cruel,* she thought. *I'm glad he was available, but I had better not tell Charles how he acted toward me.*

Now, there was nothing unusual about Emma's third pregnancy. All indications assured a robust little angel would be delivered around June thirtieth of that year. They were expecting a girl and had chosen the name, Kelly Denise Sanders. Emma was comforted as that delivery proved to be much easier than her first two, even as the sweat and tears poured forth with that one last push. Smiling, she laid back to relax. Her baby girl's wails at her first taste of a strange new world were music to Emma's ears. She raised her head and got a peek of a full head of lush curly hair and a pouty miniature face. *She had Charles' features but not his big ol' ears,* she thought with a light chuckle about to burst. Suddenly, a rasping sound from baby Kelly startled Emma. The nurse rushed to her side and swaddled the baby, but it bared little help. The baby's breathing was labored as she lost consciousness.

Emma's heart stopped as she strained to hear the sound heard only seconds before but she heard nothing.

"Doctor, what, what, what happened, ma baby stopped crying. I don't hear anything. I don't hear ma baby!" Emma was trying hard not to panic. "What's happening, where's Charles, where's ma husband?" She closed her eyes and took a deep breath. "Oh God, please take care of my baby, please help us, we need you!"

"Mrs. Sanders, Mrs. Sanders. Please try to calm yourself. We are doing everything possible for your precious daughter," Dr. Mitchell said. "She's going to be all right, please lay back and relax."

Charles was escorted into the delivery room to be with his wife while the baby was rushed next door. The doctor worked feverishly to revive her. It took about five minutes to restore her breathing. The doctor scratched his head at the sudden asphyxia. After stabilizing the struggling infant, he hurried back to the anxious parents.

Emma's tears could fill a river. "This can't be happening. This *can't* be happening. God, I don't ask ya for much, but I can't lose my baby girl. I just can't."

"Mrs. Sanders, I know you're anxious," the doctor said.

"Just tell me, what's going on? Is she okay?" Emma cried, unable to stop her tears.

Charles grabbed his wife's hand, willing himself not to break down. His wife needed him to be strong. His girls. The baby... "Tell us, doctor," Charles spoke through his clenched teeth. "Is our baby alive?"

"Yes, your baby girl is alive. She is breathing, and she is stable. However..." the doctor paused and took a deep breath. "Your daughter experienced what we call *birth asphyxia*. It's, simply put, a lack of oxygen. Sometimes we know what causes it but sometimes, I'm sorry to say, we just don't." He looked into Emma's gaping eyes. "And that's not all. Because it lasted for about five minutes, there's a strong possibility that it affected her brain..."

Emma's face dropped as the tears washed away every remembrance of her young and vibrant glow. She buried her face in her husband's chest and gave way to her sobs. Charles wrapped his strong arms around her, hoping he could keep her together through sheer force, but even he--himself--was barely hanging on.

"I'm so sorry," the doctor whispered.

"Can we see her?" Emma asked.

"Right now we have her on ventilation, and we'll be running more tests," the doctor said. "Hypoxic damage can occur in the organs as well, but the brain is the least likely candidate for a complete healing."

Emma raised her blanket over her face, unsure if she could bear any more.

The doctor touched Emma's arm, comfortingly. "Mrs. Sanders, if you would like me to come back later to finish our talk, I understand."

"No," Charles cut in. "We want to know everything. What kind of problems is our child gonna have?"

"Right now, it's too soon to tell--"

"Then, tell us the risks," Charles pressed.

The doctor hesitated but only for a moment. "Well, she's at high risk for developmental delay or an intellectual disability. There's also the possibility of seizures--"

"Stop!" Emma cried. "Let's just stop for now. I want to see my daughter, my Kelly. Can I see her?"

"You will be able to see her shortly. Please know that we are doing all we can with preventive measures to give her a fighting chance. I know you are a praying woman, Mrs. Sanders, keep praying."

As it turned out, there was some damage. The baby had breathing difficulties throughout her first year, and her speech came a little later than most her age. Cognitive concerns with comprehension and memory came in as she got older. Then anxiety attacks would enter upon too much stress. Emma prayed that baby Kelly would somehow rise and excel despite the difficulties her life would hold.

"She doesn't need therapy or medication," Emma often told family and friends. "We tried medicine and the outcome was not good. It would put her in such a stupor that she was as a dead zombie. I guess, the meds would mess with her brain cells or somethin'. There was no spark, no life in my child, at all. What good is that? So, the Lord and I will be her therapists from now on. Besides, she's not alone. She has her sisters."

Jessie, the eldest, is prim and proper as the natural born leader and protector. Tiffany, aka Tiffy, the middle girl is a teaser and somewhat mischievous.

"Girls now, we as a family are going to take turns working with Kelly until we turn every corner that needs turnin'. Your sister is not strange. She's distinctive, and that's okay. If we were all the same, it would be a boring world. There are no second-class citizens, just folk needing love is all, with no one to help 'em so they've been mislabeled. Her condition is not her fault, but we would be wrong if we gave up without a fight."

Twinges of guilt also plagued Emma, at times. She felt somewhat to blame for her daughter's condition. *Did I eat the right foods? Did I take on too much during the pregnancy? Did I do something wrong?"* she often questioned herself.

Just two years later, her pain doubled as Charles was in a car accident. He didn't survive an out of town trip, trying to make a better living for his family. Emma's intense involvement in her daughter's care became her fix from emotional pain, along with--of course--her faith in God.

Father, I can't understand what happened, but I know all things work together for good for those that love ya and are called for your purpose. I know you have a purpose in this. You didn't cause it 'cause you're a good father, and you will not fail your children. Kelly amazes me with so much strength and the grace you've already bestowed upon her. She's still here. God, what does her future hold?

CHAPTER 1

IT'S SUNDAY AFTERNOON after church service and the Sanders are relaxing in their living room. Kelly interrupts the talk of the day's sermon.

"I want to graduate college," Kelly tells her family.

Where did that come from? "If you really want to challenge yourself," Tiffy whispers in her younger sister's ear, "I'll help you find a man."

Kelly feels a rush of air being deflated from her pride as she walks away. During her teen year's she learned to put up a wall and ignore indifference from others, even from her smart-mouthed sister. Always a pretty girl, Kelly has grown into a stunning young woman with soft silky peach colored skin and a full head of curly dark brown hair. She stands tall and slim at 5'7". There is never a shortage of boys in her path until they *find out*. Memory problems coupled with sudden erratic behavior test their limits.

Despite continued attention, she is not quite ready to turn those pages in life yet. Tiring and exhausting rejection has become a part of her psyche. Kelly has placed what she calls a romantic lock on her reluctant brain. The ocean of emotion holds her key stuck at the bottom, entangled in algae and barnacles.

Her family is also very protective of her. Perhaps the iron fortress surrounding her is a little too impenetrable, but they don't want any "sly sneaky devils"--as Emma calls them--exploiting her. Nevertheless, how long could they "watch over" her? And when should they let go? As a grown woman, who are they to prolong or curtail any happiness that she could potentially find? Emma often finds herself musing over these questions. She is not a spring chicken for the silver strands had taken over a long time ago. It's much too early and the wrinkles are a little more visible than before, but vanity is the least of her concerns.

Her next focus is the pitter-patter of little feet before she's too old. None of her girls fare well in the relationship department. Tiffy is constantly choosing men who mean her no good, and Jessie acts as if she is not interested at all. Perhaps, it is the lack of a father figure in their life. Her brother, Uncle Terry as everyone calls him, does his best to step in when needed. However, long-distance truck driving is not easy on him or his time.

"I have a strong desire to do this thing," Kelly insists. "No one else in this family has earned a degree, so I'm going to do it. An online, non-traditional degree in Liberal arts is going to be my route and that's that!"

Tiffy gulps as she scrutinizes her sister. An unnerved look of anxiety crosses the face of her mother and Jessie.

"I've been reading about the curriculum. I can do it. I want to try. Will you all help me?" Kelly begs.

The Sanders have no idea what an online college degree would entail, but they are committed to helping her. If she is determined, then they are committed.

Jessie is the first one to break the silence. "Sister, between my work at the Post Office, I guess I can find some time to see how it works and get you started."

"Yes, you know I will help as well. It doesn't make any sense, huh, working at Jackson State all these years and not completing my degree at no cost. I know, I know, you have been telling me that all these years, Momma," Tiffy laments.

I have a feeling this is not going to be easy for her or us.

Kelly starts the process at full speed with late nights studying, on-campus visits, memory tests and the not to be forgotten financial strain on the family. The entire family's sacrifice begins to wear on her psyche. She wants to quit, but Momma and Jessie will not have it. Tiffy, on the other hand, grumbles her way through it.

"You're not a quitter, Kelly. You got this," Jesse encourages. "So what if you have had to take a few classes twice. Didn't you say you could do it? And didn't we say we would help? It's hard on us all, but it will be worth it in the end. You'll see, right Tiffy?"

Tiffy grumbles. "Right."

Her main concern is retaining the information. Her sisters help her organize her thoughts for the college level coursework. It takes longer and is more difficult than everyone could imagine. But indeed she meets her goal. The frustration with much joy pays off. Tiffy and Jessie proclaim they've earned honorary degrees as well with all they have learned. Kelly is so proud of herself, but little does she realize that moving forward at the right time yields manifold blessings.

CHAPTER 2

J ACK RILEY'S LIFE has been one of an upper-middle
class. The racially mixed area of Heatherton Estates
is the place he calls home. His family moved there
when he was about 9-years-old. He's as handsome as
they come but so modest and unassuming—an African
American man standing tall and slim at 6'2" with
close-shaved hair. There is a distinguished touch of
grey around the edges. The grey has come much too
early, at the age of 28. His light-brown eyes could melt
any woman's heart. Modeling or entertainment could
have been his calling, but none of those things moved
him. His heart is in a different place. His older brother,
Carter, took after their father and was of a tall and
stocky build.

Growing up, Jack was always an inquisitive and knowledge-thirsty child who developed an unusual sensitivity to the needs of other people. Toy trucks were not in his vocabulary but put a colorful picture book in front of him, and he would point to every character and give them a play name. "Mommy, that's my friend Benny and he's hungry."

"Yes Jack, that's Benny. Let's give him some food, okay?" said his mother to her amusement.

His father, Antonio, often took Jack and Carter to his old childhood neighborhood to remind his sons of where he came from and how far they had come, by grace. They would hang out with neighbors and listen to their stories of struggles and perseverance. Those moments left a lasting impression on Jack as he found the old economic and educational struggles still existed in the old neighborhood.

Antonio, now sixty-seven, has been sidelined with health issues for most of his life. Along with congestive heart failure, hip problems leave him confined to a wheelchair at times. This curtails his long held dream of holding a political office, taking a toll on him mentally. Nevertheless, with his wife's encouragement, he launches out into the world of real estate. Finding enjoyment and a newfound passion, he is able to build multiple streams of income from his holdings. However, he still hoped one of his sons would take up the call of social injustice. And one of them did. Jack majored in political science, earning a master's degree in public policy. Carter, on the other hand, answered the call of duty as a physician. He works at a medical clinic in one of Jackson's underserved neighborhoods. Antonio and Laurie Riley are proud parents as their sons have pursued their life long dreams of making a difference.

Graduation day at Jackson State has arrived for Kelly Sanders, and the relentless rain has finally stopped. For two long days, the town took a severe spring beating. However, on this morning, the sun burst through as bright and overpowering as the rain had been. Kelly takes it as a sign for her accomplishment during the last five years. Being part of the on-campus ceremony is a dream come true.

The administrators ask if Kelly would like to say a few words for a special honor of perseverance and achievement. Though she practiced a limited speech, she is not prepared to proceed with it. Her nerves are too jittery. She thought she could do it but her palms are sweating, and her hands are shaking too much. She looks down at her speech--good thing she wrote it down. Maybe it won't be so bad. One glance at her sisters and they smile back. She focuses in on her mom's lips as she mouths. *You can do this, Kelly. You can do this.*

Kelly stands and walks to the podium. Over 2,000 faces stare back at her. She's drenching in sweat. A minute passes before one of the administrators moves toward her for reassurance. Before he touches her shoulder, her mouth opens.

"Tha, tha, thank you so much. My fam-family deserves this just as much. I, I, do. I could not have done this without God, my family and the faculty." Her mouth is still vibrating, but no other words can be coaxed. As Kelly walks off the stage, the crowd is dead silent.

Tiffy springs up to get the ball rolling. "My girl, yeah! Way to go! You did good, sister!"

"Yeah," cries Uncle Terry, boisterously as he rises.

"My baby earned a college degree. Who would have thought this 15-years-ago, but by the grace of God!" cries Emma in her seat. "This is one of the proudest moments of my life!" She hugs Uncle Terry with blissful joy. But something more magical, and unimaginable, is still yet in store.

The day's events are pretty overwhelming and exhausting. After pictures with family and friends, Kelly requests a quick bite to eat before going to bed. She and the family drive to her favorite restaurant.

"Kelly, are you sure you don't want to head to Uptown Night's?" Jessie asks. "It's a nicer venue. It's a big day for you. You deserve it."

"Nope, I want *Julia's House.*"

"Dang, I got all dressed to the nines for nothing," fumes Tiffy.

Kelly knew her sisters didn't care for the $6.99 mashed potatoes and cheap steak, dinner special. But Kelly liked simple--she took after her mother in that way--and since it was her day, she wanted *Julia's House.*

Arriving at the small diner, the girls push their way through a large crowd. The restaurant is never that crowded. They look out the window, across the street is Simmons' Park, and the group is even larger there.

"What's going on? Tiffy asks a nearby patron.

"Jack Riley is holding a campaign rally," the patron replies.

In 2002, Riley set his sights on a seat in the congressional office of his state as a house representative. The death of one of the district incumbents has called for a special election. After sliding through the nominating process of the Democratic Party, he wins the primary election, but the fight has only begun and he knows it. The general election is now in sight.

He started his political life as a city council member in his district. He is an extremely personable and charismatic hands-on alderman who made himself available and accountable to his constituents. His goal is to bring back honesty and integrity to the office. A daunting task he knows, but if he can at least start changing in the right direction, then his efforts will not have been in vain. He is no shrinking flower in city council; thus, when he speaks his colleagues listen as there is an uncanny magnetism. People believe in his call to office. Based on his past, he demonstrated effective leadership, and now is the time to run for a higher office. He is encouraged to move forward and capture on the momentum.

Jack's platform of transparency and integrity has gained tremendous ground. He seems to be making much headway ahead of his opponent, Clark Donovan Hester. The old regime lives on in his opponent Mr. Hester, who has been in politics much longer than Jack.

"Look! That's Jack Riley over there in the park," exclaims Tiffy. "Let's go see!"

"Since when are you into politics?" Jessie asks.

"He's so attractive, who cares what he has to say." Tiffy smiles and Jessie laughs. "You know me. I like to tell it like it is and like it ain't, sometimes. Maybe I should run for office!"

They all laugh.

"Woman, behave yourself and settle down now," says Emma.

"Well, I've been following his campaign and he talks a good game, anyone would be better than Clark at the moment. He certainly has my vote," Jessie says.

The girls push their way out of the diner and across the street to the park. They stand in the back as Jack continues his speech.

"Well, as you all can perceive from that famous statement, I am certainly no Jack Kennedy but..." Laughter is heard from the audience. "I am Jack Riley, not a copy of anyone else."

"Let's move a little closer so I can hear him better," says Jessie.

They move as far to the front of the platform as they are allowed. His speech is short on this day as he closes.

"Well, you can vote for the same, or you can vote for the change. I'm not into tricks or treats to gain your confidence. The people in this district are smart. They know when they have been had. Let's get this done! Thank you for listening and voting for change."

As he begins to converse and shake the hands of his constituents, the crowd demands that he takes a few questions. He stated earlier that his schedule would not allow it.

"Well, there you have it, another lying politician," Emma mumbles. "How many of them do what they actually spew forth? Let's go. We've heard this nonsense before."

"But you gotta admit, Momma," Tiffy says with a smile. "Isn't he good looking?"

"Not as good looking as yo' daddy was," Emma chuckles.

"Apples and oranges, Ma." Jessie rolls her eyes.

"Come on, let's greet him!" Tiffy begs. "Let's get in

that line. It's not too long. This may be the only chance we get to meet him. Heck, he may be our next president!"

"Oh, all right." Emma surrenders. "I guess I did call the poor man a lying politician. The least I could do is shake his hand."

The ladies giggle just as Jack reaches them.

"Thank you for coming, I need your vote," he says as he shakes Tiffy, Jessie and Emma's hands. Kelly steps back and turns away sheepishly just as he extends his hand. His eyes light up as he interprets her body language as a brush off. He looks curiously at her, but she looks away as if hiding her eyes from his gaze. Intrigued, he steps in front of her.

"Did I say something to offend you?" he asks, searching for her eyes.

"Your speech," Kelly says. "Momma says we heard it all before." Lowering her voice even softer, "and putting it mildly, you're probably dishonest."

Jack laughs. "Well, I can assure you. I'm different."

"How can we be sure of that?" Kelly asks, finally looking up to meet his eyes. The softness of her gaze leaves Jack speechless. Not only was she stunningly beautiful, but brutally honest.

"I guess, I will just have to prove it." Jack extends his hand to her again. "I'm Jack."

"I know who you are."

"You do?" Jack asks, surprised.

"Yes." Kelly nods, pointing at the large banner

above the stage. "Your name is everywhere, and I can read."

Jack laughs, but before he has a chance to respond, the crowd breaks into a roar.

"We want Jack! We want Jack! We want Jack!"

His younger aide, Tony O'Neil, pulls him aside. "I think it would be good business if you adjusted your schedule and answered a few questions right about now."

"Okay, fine." Jack surrenders. "But I need a favor. I need you to follow that family over there walking away and stall them just a bit until I finish here. I won't be long. I'll explain later."

"Are you serious?"

While Jack heads back to the platform, mumbling under his breath regarding his newfound duties, Tony sees the family entering the diner and goes after them. Seated in the crowded restaurant, the Sanders girls are looking over their selections when Tony approaches them.

"Hello, good people. My name is Tony O'Neil, and I work with Mr. Riley. I do apologize for disturbing your dinner. I only need a moment of your time, if I may. I noticed you listening to his speech, but as you walked away he was about to take a few questions. I'm just here for a quick assessment, survey or whatever you want to call it."

Emma raises her eyeglasses and glares at him.

"Oh boy, okay, I'll be quick. So, what do you think of

Jack Riley's platform for change?" he asks.

"Well, I understand he's an accomplished councilman, and from what I've been continually hearing, he holds great promise as one of our state reps," Emma asserts. "Now you tell me, in what part of the world has anyone not been hearing about change, more jobs, a better economy and how they plan to make it work? I have been living in Jackson all my life, and quite frankly, it doesn't matter who's in office, I know who holds the future. I wish him the best in his fight for change, and if he wins, he has our prayers and the prayers of many 'cause he's gonna need them. Now, if you'll excuse us, we need to order our meals."

Tiffy's jaw stiffens trying to hold back her amusement.

"Well, hmm, there was a compliment in there somewhere, I think," Tony replies. "We truly believe that Jack Riley could be a breath of fresh air for the people, unlike his opponent."

"Of course, you do. That's what they pay you for." Emma smiles. "Now, if you excuse us, we're ready to order."

"Right. Well, thank you for your kind and honest words ma'am." Tony glances over his shoulder and looks across the street. He scans through the crowd searching for Jack. "Hmmm, yeah ugh, how about that new computer warehouse they're building on the outskirts of Triton? Did you know Jack had a hand in that?"

Emma puts her menu down and looks up at him again. "Why are you really here, Mr. Tony?"

"Okay, fine. You and your family caught Mr. Riley's attention. He asked me to stall you."

"Why did he ask you to do that?" Emma asks.

"Is he that desperate for votes?" Tiffy teases as she giggles with Jessie.

"Very funny." Tony turns his attention back to Emma. "I wish I knew more, ma'am. Although..." He steals a quick glance at Kelly who was still looking over the menu. "I have a wild guess, and I'm sure you do, too."

Tiffy and Jessie look at their mother with eyes widened. "Did he just say--"

"Why, hello again!" Jack appears with a wide smile as Tony's color returns to his face. Jack looks at Emma. "I'm sorry for interrupting your dinner. Please, allow it to be my treat."

Emma responds with a cordial nod. "Thank you, Mr. Riley."

"Please, call me Jack," he says, offering his hand. "You have a beautiful family, Mrs... and I can see where they get their looks from."

Boy, ain't he full of baloney, Emma thinks. "I'm Mrs. Sanders, and these are my three daughters, Jessie, Tiffy, and Kelly."

"Hi ladies, how are you today?" Jack greets Tiffy and Jessie with a polite nod, but with a swift movement of the eyes, he turns to face Kelly--his stare is intense and with no shame.

Kelly flashes a smile. "Hi, uh, uh, it's great, I mean, nice to meet you."

A noticeable flash of rosy pink appears across her cheeks as she lowers her head in embarrassment. There's a flutter of anticipation in this man's presence, such as she's never experienced before. She wonders if it's because of the grand drama surrounding him-- the supposed celebrity status along with her imagination. Unless it wasn't. Could it be something more?

Moving closer to the edge of the table, Tiffy stares him down unashamedly until Emma nudges her to behave. Kelly senses he's somewhat different and immediately feels a non-judgmental ease in his presence. Her sense of sweetness and innocence appeals to him. Most of the women he meets practically throw themselves at him, or he finds them too bossy and demanding for his taste.

Immediately understanding his intent, Emma clears her throat. "You're here because of my daughter, am I right Mr. Riley?"

Shrugging his shoulders, he adjusts his shirt collar, trying to calculate the right words to use before opening his mouth. "I meant no disrespect, Mrs. Sanders. I was just very drawn to her. Is she not of legal age?"

"Yes, she is. In fact, tonight we're celebrating her graduation," Emma says, motioning toward Kelly. "She earned a BA degree, and we are so proud."

"Wow, outstanding." Jack looks at Kelly. "Congratulations."

"Thank you," Kelly replies, blushing.

"I'll be very brief, and I do apologize again for disturbing your dinner," Jack says. "I can only imagine how important this celebration is for you all."

"I don't think you can quite imagine, Mr. Riley, how it is indeed a very worthy celebration," says Emma.

"Well, I'm so glad I could have a little part in this," Jack says with a smile. "I just wanted to introduce myself as a candidate, and yes, you were right to the other motive..." His eyes dart toward Kelly, again. "I would be honored if I could have the pleasure of speaking with you at a future time."

Emma holds her peace.

"May I please have your number?" Jack asks, handing Kelly one of his cards. "You can write it on the back of my card here. I'd like to give you a call. Perhaps we can talk?"

To Jack's amusement, Jessie and Tiffy quickly hand Jack their house number before Kelly could finish writing.

"It's okay Jack, we all live together, we have the same number," says Tiffy, laughing.

"Mr. Riley." Emma waits for Jack to look at her. "My daughter is a very special person."

"I believe that." Jack turns to Kelly one last time. "I truly do." He doesn't know what it is yet, but he already senses a deep connection. He beams.

"Thank you for your precious time. Enjoy your meal and have a great rest of your day." He leaves smiling, and Tony follows.

Lowering her eyeglasses, Emma studies her daughter, hoping she does not read too much into what just happened. Kelly is smiling and twirling her curls around her fingers. Tiffy and Jessie gaze at her, too.

"What?" Kelly asks, "Why are you all looking at me?"

Jack and Tony stand outside the diner, talking. The acrid smell of cigarette smoke wafts up Jack's nose, irritating him.

"Man, I'm glad you showed up when you did," Tony says, holding a cigarette between his lips. "Those women were hard to stall."

"Tony, you need to let those cigarettes go before they hurt you," Jack tells him.

"I'm trying man, but don't change the subject. That lady was testing you big time. You need to leave her daughter alone before you end up on the 6 o'clock news for another reason. You know Hester would be all over that, trying to pin any little thing on you."

Jack laughs. "Hester can do whatever he wants to

do."

Tony sighs. "You gotta let this go, man. Right now is the worst possible time to get distracted."

"I wish I could," Jack confesses. "There's something about her that's drawing me--a special innocence I've never seen before. It's as if I can see into her soul a longing to be loved, protected, and valued. I've met a lot of women, but this one is calling me."

CHAPTER 3

THE SANDERS' SMALL kitchen table is abuzz with activity as the girls wait for Kelly to come out of her room. Tiffy has finished cooking pancakes as the ladies help themselves. Emma keeps a large artificial plant in the middle of the table taking most of the space. It's a replica of one that Charles gave her when they first met; she ensures everyone is careful with it.

Tiffy strategically places the main dish, the butter, and the syrup around the plant, mumbling, "Let it go, Ma. Let it go."

"If you touch that plant, it's you and me," Emma declares. "You can dust, though."

Tiffy grumbles.

There is much banter as the family talk about the

chance meeting with Jack Riley and his seeming interest in Kelly. They believe nothing could ever develop between the two of them and chuckle at even the thought.

"Sure he's well-known, single, and very good-looking. But he's still a politician which means he's image conscious," Jessie says wolfing down another bite. "Hey, nice and fluffy Tiff. Good job but you gotta be able to cook more than pancakes."

"Yes, not bad baby," Emma laughs.

"Ha, ha, ha, cute Jessie, but anyway yeah, you know all he wants is eye candy on his arm. Kelly is eye candy, but he and my sis would not be on the same page," Tiffy says, firmly.

"Watch your mouth, Tiffy," Emma glares. "Your sister is a lot more than that. She's the smartest woman in this house. They don't hand out degrees like Halloween candy. She worked hard, and she earned it. The point is—whatever his intentions are, he will not take advantage of your sister."

Kelly finally enters the kitchen and all chatter ceases. She is unaware they have been gabbing about her. Nevertheless, she doubts herself, as well. As much as she wishes she could relive yesterday one more time... *Oh, well!*

"Okay ladies, I've got to get to the nursing home early today. They changed my shift. Tiffy, since you have a day off, how 'bout you pull that roast out of the freezer and prove yourself, tonight? There's some white potatoes in the bin and add some frozen vegetables on the side, okay?"

"Everyone will be licking their chops tonight. I promise. My last boyfriend enjoyed my cooking," Tiffy brags.

"No wonder he never came back," Jessie teases, and Kelly laughs.

"You've got a lot of nerve, Jessie. But that's all right, at least I can count the number of boyfriends I've had on two hands. Do you know the number of hands on a clock? It's two, right? Yes, two. And that's the number of men that have called you in the last three years."

"You did not just go there." Jessie's face hardens.

"Oh, I did." Tiffy glares back. "And who gets tickets for driving tooooo slooooww? Why, Jessie Marie Sanders of course, that's who!"

"Oh, you wanna go there?" Jessie yells. "I've got some secrets that can be told right here and now since we're in a run of the mouth mood. Shall I continue, shall I? Keep talking. I dare you, now."

Taking one last bite of bacon, Kelly grabs her half-eaten plate and hurries out of the room. She is torn between hearing secrets or saving her fragile nerves. Her nerves win.

"Ladies, ladies. Stop acting like children. Y'all upsetting your sister, which despite being the youngest, is the only one with sense right now." Emma looks at Tiffy. "The number of boyfriends you have is not a measure of your worth or something to take pride in. I'm tired of telling you that. God alone determines your worth. Get your mind on God's will for your life, and he will send you a good man. Now, I have to get ready for work."

Jack has every intention of following through on his promise. He waits several days before making the call. He's still puzzled, however, by the strange reaction from Kelly's mother. Why was she so protective of Kelly?

The phone rings late one night and Tiffy answers.

"Hello, good evening, this is Jack Riley, your new favorite politician," he jokes. "May I speak with Kelly Sanders, please?"

"Oh hi, Mr. Riley! How are you?" *Oh my, he called.*

"I am great, who am I speaking with?"

"This is Tiffany Sanders, but you can call me Tiffy."

"How are you, Tiffy?"

"I'm great."

"Good to hear. Now, may I speak with Kelly, please?"

Holding her hand over the phone receiver, she whispers to her sister standing nearby. "Are you available *Miss Kelly Sanders* to take a call?" She grins, being silly.

"Who is it?" Kelly asks.

She drops the phone by accident, picks it up and tries to hand it to Kelly, but Kelly refuses to take it.

"Who is it? Kelly asks a second time.

"Take a wild guess."

"Is it, is it, uh, oh my, is it who I, I, I think it is?" Kelly stutters, feeling warm as her pulse quickens. The women look at each other. Kelly paces back and forth slowly rubbing her hands down the sides of her neck.

"He actually called me." Kelly couldn't believe it. "He's, he's like, he's like a celebrity!"

Tiffy places her hand back over the phone receiver.

"Girl, he probably heard you, and no, Kelly, he's, he's like a man, just a man!" Tiffy laughs, mocking her.

Kelly rubs her clammy hands over her pants before finally grabbing the phone.

"Geez, just relax, take a deep breath," Jessie encourages from across the room.

"Hellooo, Mr. Riley. Uh, I mean... Hi, Mr. Riley," Kelly responds before heading off to her bedroom for privacy.

"Hey sis, ask about Tony for me?" shouts Tiffy before Kelly disappears and slams the door.

"Why do you sound so nervous, Kelly?" Jack asks on the other line. "I can sense an uneasiness. You don't have to be afraid of me. I'm just your average Joe in an expensive suit trying to make a difference, that's all. Don't like wearin' em but they come with the position."

"Joe, I thought your name was Jack," Kelly jokes, snickering.

They both laugh.

"See, I'm easy," Jack says, amused by her sense of humor.

"Okay, but I'm still uneasy," Kelly confesses.

"Well, it's alright. It'll pass, hopefully," he says with a light chuckle. "First of all, I'd like to thank you for taking my call. "I think you are a very beautiful woman, but it's more than just the physical. There's something different about you, not quite sure what is it, yet."

Yeah, there's something different about me alright. "Thank you, Mr. Riley."

"Please, call me Jack."

"Jack..." She likes the sound of it which makes her even more uneasy. He doesn't know anything about her, and she's not quite sure she wants him to. "So, why politics?"

"Well, we all have a mission and purpose in life, and I believe this is straight and narrow at the moment. Seriously, though, I'd like to bring some healing and change to ailments of society, economic, social and spiritual. I would probably need to take the challenge higher for that spiritual nod," he muses. "I don't intend to be in politics all my life. As I certainly don't enjoy being called a crook or a liar as your mother so kindly put it."

Kelly laughs. "Mama can be quite blunt sometimes

but don't--don't worry. I'm sure not everyone thinks that."

"What do you think?" Jack asks, intrigued. "Do you think I'm a crook and a liar?"

"Hmm, let me see, as a kid did your momma ever leave her purse lying around unattended?"

"Well, yeah. Why?"

"Did you ever take something out of it that was probably a little larger than a nickel?" Kelly asks.

Jack smiles. "I might have taken a quarter, once."

"Did you lie about taking it when asked where you got the money for that candy?"

Jack grins. "Maybe."

"Then, I guess that makes you a crook and a liar, Jack."

His laughter is magic to her ears. "Okay, fine. You got me there," he says, still laughing. "But would it help if I told you that I've paid her back since then?"

Kelly giggles, cheerfully. She cannot believe how much more at ease she now feels. She lies down and stretches out across her bed.

"Besides," Jack goes on. "I think everyone's done that."

"Perhaps, but we're only talking about you right now."

Jack laughs again, and the sound makes Kelly relax.

"You're funny," he says, surprised.

Kelly smiles. "I enjoy talking with you." She suddenly hears a noise outside her door and turns to look. The shadow underneath gives her sister away. Are both of them eavesdropping or just Tiffy?

"Well, now it's your turn, Miss Kelly," Jack says. "Tell me about you."

"What do you want to know?" she asks, trying to keep herself from sharing too much, too soon.

"Well, you just graduated, didn't you?" he asks. "What's your degree?"

Computer Science, Math, Psychology... those were the words she wish would come out of her mouth, but she doesn't want to lie. "I have a degree in the Arts."

"Really, you're an artist?"

"No, not that one. The other one, the well-rounded degree, the more Liberal one."

They both chuckle.

"Hey, that's still outstanding. That's obviously the one that will take you far in your mission and purpose, right? So, what *is* your mission and purpose, Miss Kelly?"

The phone shakes in her hand as she starts stuttering. "Uh, uh, uh, uh." The idea of explaining a purpose for her life leaves her stumped. She has no long-range goal that's worth celebrating. She feels doubt and limitations starting to flood her brain. Making a good impression is all she wants, but her mind suddenly blanks out. Her sixth-grade classroom comes to mind. The children laughing as she tries to make a transition from special ED to a regular room. Children tripping her as she walks home. Never ending jokes about her intelligence in high school. It all comes rushing back, and she suddenly starts to feel overwhelmed. She sits up quickly and presses her back against the bed frame.

Despite her family continually reassuring her that she is as good and intelligent as anyone, Kelly still feels the fear of failure overpowering her senses. Her wires are crossing and freezing, and although her mouth is open, she can't get any word out. For a brief moment, she had forgotten she was speaking with someone so intelligent and polished. And with a blink of an eye, her confidence vanishes.

"Kelly, are you alright?" Jack asks. "You're making a clicking sound with your voice. Did I say something wrong?"

"Ohhh, I have to get off the phone."

"Why?"

"I don't want to talk anymore."

"Kelly, what's wrong?"

"I have to get off the phone. I have to get off the phone."

"Okay, okay." His pulse begins to rise along with hers. "It's okay, just calm down. Take a deep breath."

He listens to her soft rhythmic breathing as she settles herself.

"I'm so sorry, Jack," she says, catching her breath. "I won't waste any more of your time. It was nice talking to you. I wish you the best."

"Wait, don't hang up, please!" Jack begs. "I would

like to see you. Can I visit you tomorrow? I would really like to."

Kelly doesn't respond. She wants to, but she's not sure what to say.

Jack goes on before she could turn him down. "How about I stop by around seven?"

"Umm…" Kelly rocks back and forth, nervously. "Okay. First house on the left as you enter the London Town complex." She hangs up quickly and slams the phone down.

Her sisters are anxiously waiting for her to open the door. Kelly bolts out of her room drenched in sweat.

"Here she comes," announces Jessie.

"Her face will tell us everything we need to know," Tiffy says.

"What happened to you, are you feeling sick?" her mother asks. "Sit down, sweetheart. What happened?"

"He, he wants, he wants, he wants to come see me tomorrow evening," she blurts out. "I can't believe it."

"Neither can I," Tiffy mumbles under her breath. "Are you sure you can handle this?"

Kelly shakes her head, her palms still sweating.

"Oh, great." Tiffy rolls her eyes. "This just keeps getting better and better."

"Be nice, Tiffy," Jessie says. "This could be something we all have to accept and get used to."

"Yeah right," Tiffy grumbles.

"Watch your mouth, missy," Emma interjects after

taking it all in. "Sure, let him come over, I want to talk to him."

As Kelly gets up to head to her room, Tiffy blurts out. "Don't worry, after this meeting, it ain't going nowhere!"

Though Emma secretly prays that someday such a thing could happen to her baby, she can't imagine Jack being the one for her.

CHAPTER 4

THE GRANDPARENTING tug has intensified in Jack's mother, Laurie. She's becoming overly concerned as to the marital status of her sons. She wants both to marry—or in Carter's case, to remarry. After his divorce, he declared it would be a long time before he walked that path again. She desires grandchildren sooner rather than later. Carter has step-children, Ray who's twelve and Donovan, fourteen--but Laurie doesn't get to see them much. "Find a wife; you both need to find wives," Laurie hounded constantly.

Jack has had plenty of dates being both handsome and charismatic. Carter too, being a single doctor and all. But none of the relationships fare better than trying to light a match on a windy night.

"Where did we go wrong, Antonio?" Laurie asked her husband at every mention of another failed relationship.

"You need to stop fretting about it," Antonio replies. "If I know your red-blooded sons, it will happen. Leave it alone woman. There's nothing wrong! Just be glad one of them is still here."

Laurie feels troubled. "What are you talking about, what does that mean?" she asks, nervously.

"It just means you were about to lose Carter a couple of times by my hands around his neck. His attitude is fierce at times. Must be from your side of the family."

They both laugh.

Jack's mother has tried taking matchmaking into her own hands. As a former school-teacher and sales rep., she has a vast network of friends. Jack never seems interested in the accomplished women introduced to him by his mom. Not having the time was the answer he stuck with. Laurie knows to stay away from Carter with her match-making skills. He has no tolerance for it.

On the evening before his visit with Kelly, Jack's at his parents' home. Laurie sees him all dressed up and cannot pass up the opportunity to bring up the subject.

"Jack, honey, you're too darn picky," she says. "Do you even give women a chance to hold your interest?

You've met a lot of wonderful Christian women. Looking for perfection, are we?"

"No, actually, I'm not looking for perfection, quite the opposite. But I must admit that in the beginning, I was. Then, I realized I wasn't all that perfect, either. Imagine that!" He grins. "I'm trying to concentrate on this office right now. So, I'll just step back and let God do his thing. He will lead me to the one he has for me, 'cause you know, I called many, but few were chosen!"

He and his mom laugh.

"Boy, you're so silly. Don't twist the word of God like that. Hush up!" says Laurie as she finishes making a pot of stew.

"Alright, alright. I've been stalling in your good 'ol kitchen, waiting to bag up some of your famous vittles then I'm heading on home," Jack says.

"Well, when you find the right one, I'll give her my good 'ol home cooking recipe!" Laurie smirks. "Better yet, you're a pretty good chef. Try this one yourself."

"Mom, don't fret yourself over my love life. Que sera, sera!"

"Well honey, your dad and I aren't getting any younger."

"I'm going to give you and dad at least one crumb snatcher, okay now?" He walks out the door with stew in hand.

"Well, a wife better come with it," she hollers as he leaves.

Jack stops and turns around to face his mother. "I

may have a surprise for you, Mom. Just be patient."

Her eyes light up. She quits her fussing and finally takes the matter to the Lord in prayer. As she is praying, "Lord, I've been blessed with two fine sons who you gave the grace of making a difference in this world. Antonio and I are so thankful for that. I know I've been kind of hounding them both to find wives 'cause I would like some grandchildren before I get too old. I hope that doesn't sound too selfish. Lord, can you please make that happen? Help them to find good, virtuous women, please. I'm finally giving it to you."

Laurie then heard in her spirit, *"I've been waiting for you to finally come to me. Take your hands off of it."*

CHAPTER 5

JACK ENTERS LONDON TOWN and parks in front of the Sanders' home. It's a small, modest, well-kept bi-level. All the homes in the subdivision are cookie cutter with different colored brick facings.

The Sanders' red brick home stands out with beautiful multi-colored flowers and plants lining the front porch. No doubt Mrs. Sanders' touch as he wonders if Kelly has as good a green thumb as her mother. Two neighbors are sitting on the porch next door. They stare him down as he walks to the door. Smiling and waving at them does not incite the move of a hand or jaw muscle in return. *Wow, friendly neighbors. The Neighborhood Watch, I suppose.* As his finger presses the doorbell, one of the neighbor's calls out.

"Hey, Jack Riley right? I thought so, took me a minute though. Can I talk to ya on ya way out?"

Jack chuckles. "Sure, sir."

Emma receives him at the door and invites him to take a seat. *Lord help me to explain my daughter to this man.*

"It's nice to see you again, Mrs. Sanders. How have you been? How are things?"

"Very well, Mr. Riley. Welcome to our humble abode." Emma waves him inside. "How are you? How is the campaign going?"

"I'm well, and I know I'd have a good chance of winning with good people like you pulling for me." He laughs.

Emma looks at him, seriously. "Well, I might vote for you."

He coughs. "That's all I can ask for. Thank you, is Kelly available?"

"Yes, she is, but I would like to have a little talk with you first if you don't mind."

"Oh, okay sure."

Emma walks him to the sofa. "Mr. Riley, it's nice that you have taken an interest in my daughter, but I think I need to tell you a few things. Please, have a seat. I don't want you to be misinformed from the get-go. My lovely brave daughter is a special woman. She was deprived of oxygen at birth, and she's suffered some consequences as a result. I'll just be honest with you and not hold back. She suffers from mental lapses, anxiety, and at times you may find her stuttering. But despite all of that she is quite intelligent. You may never know how she will respond under certain conditions."

"Would it alright if I asked what conditions you are referring to, Ms. Sanders?" Jack asks, carefully.

"Well, they can vary, but she's known to become a little...well, for lack of a better word, unstable at times—especially when under severe emotional stress. But as I said before, she functions pretty well under most circumstances."

Jack finds himself speechless. He wasn't expecting something of this nature, but thinking back to the incident from the night before, now it made sense.

"May I please ask you if she's on...on some type of medication?" he sheepishly asks.

Emma knows he has no right to this information, but she believes that perhaps the answer will send him packing. With eyes bucked, Emma asserts, "Not anymore. I don't want her drugged up and in a stupor, she doesn't need it. The meds didn't agree with her body."

Jack looks bewildered but doesn't head for the door. Emma keeps talking to persuade him that it would be in his best interest, and Kelly's too, if he were to leave.

"I'm not a perfect mother and I know I can be overprotective at times, but Kelly is the one I really gotta keep my eye on. So, I know you wanna get on with your very public life. You've got something really big coming up. So sorry I had to hit you with this as soon as you walked through the door, but I think it was the best thing to do. I can see you out now."

Emma heads toward the door, but Jack doesn't follow. It's as if his feet are literally stuck to the floor.

"Mr. Riley, for what possible reason could you still be sitting there?" asserts Emma.

He delays speaking for a moment. "Ma'am, I understand your concerns, and I'm sorry that happened to your daughter. To be honest, why I'm still here defies me as well but believe me, my intentions are good."

"And just what are your intentions?" Emma asks. "You are in politics, seeking an even higher office. I honestly don't believe you would be a good fit for her. You wouldn't have time for my daughter and her needs. So, why start something you can't finish? Are you just trying to take advantage of her vulnerability? I won't let that happen. I won't let you hurt her!"

Wow. He ponders a bit before voicing his opinion. "Ma'am, your daughter is not a little girl or a monster. Sounds like you don't believe she is capable of engaging with another human being on an intimate and deeper level. As I was speaking with her yesterday, I found her quite engaging, funny, and intelligent enough to hold her own. I think you're selling your own daughter short. I'd like to talk with her some more and get to know her better. And it may help you to know that I make time for what I want."

The lines on Emma's face are more pronounced than ever. Her hands grasp her hips as she sucks in her breath.

"Now, who do you think you are talking to me about my own flesh and blood, my child. I know you are well known in this city, but you are a stranger in this house. Now you're telling me you know more about the woman I gave birth to, that I fed and clothed, that I cried many nights over, that I taught to pray? "

Jack bows his head. He knows he has gone too far. "Ma'am please, please forgive me. I am sorry, I meant no disrespect. I know I'm only on the outside looking in and I know very little about your daughter."

"You've got that right!" Emma snaps back.

"You're right, she is special, and I wouldn't trust her with just anyone, either. But with all due respect, why not let her feel free to explore and enjoy life and possibly find that there is another brighter world that is waiting for her. I have heard everything you've said, but I hope it's not too presumptuous of me to ask you to trust me? It is possible that I may see Kelly differently? Just maybe?" Managing to crack a smile, he looks at her. "Do you think that could, well, be a reasonable assumption?"

Emma is not amused as they stare at each other.

Seconds pass as he is the first to turn away. Her face softens; *he may have a point, but I won't give him the pleasure of voicing my changing thoughts, at least not yet.*

Kelly enters the room, putting a stop to their conversation. She smiles brightly with the intention of looking confident considering her last conversation with Jack.

Jack tries to put the previous night behind him. "I'd like to speak with your daughter in private," Jacks says to Emma. "I hope that's okay."

"Only for a moment."

"Would you like to sit outside on the porch, Kelly?" he asks.

She obliges. He thinks to himself *so far, so good.* Kelly is at her best again and is very charming and witty. He doesn't want a repeat of the past night, so he tries to keep the conversation veered in a particular direction and let Kelly take the lead.

"I feel sort of at ease talking to you," she confesses.

"Good, that's what I want." Jack smiles, relieved. "You know your mom was telling me that--"

"So, so, so do you really think you will win the election?"

Jack notices her change in subject and decides to follow along. "Well, I don't want to get ahead of myself. I don't pay much attention to polls because we all know they can be wrong. So, we will have to wait and see."

"You know, I would like to bring change to the world somehow as well, in a way only I can. I want to leave my mark," she says.

Oh great, now if I could only keep her talking about herself, get inside.

"What would you like the world to say about you, Miss Kelly?"

Kelly's eyes soften. She's never been asked that before. An overwhelming feeling of emotion washes over her as she pauses to reflect. "Hmm, well, honestly Jack, that I am an overcomer, accomplished, and that I am enough. But mostly, that I matter--that there is more to me than what meets the eye. That I am a believer and I have faith to become what God created me to be despite what others think. I am a Christian, Jack. My faith is very important to me, and I know you are a Christian, as well."

"Yes. I couldn't have made it as far as I have, without him." Jack agrees. "And I want to get to know you because you *do* matter. And I am so glad you feel comfortable with me to open yourself up like this. You know there are people out there who feel you don't deserve to live life to the fullest. That you're not worthy. But that's not true. I heard a preacher say once that we're seeking approval from people who don't know they're approved, so they can't really give it to us. Some of us have a natural tendency to magnify the negative; thus we will do and say anything possible to keep a person where we think they should be—simply because we're not like them."

"Why do you think that is?" Kelly asks.

"It stems from insecurity, and if you feel negative about yourself, people will pick up on those vibes and try to keep you in that vein. There are many things God has taught me that I had kind of gotten away from but they're being brought back to my spirit. You're bringing them back to me. The preacher in me is coming out," he exclaims, grinning. "I can only add to what you've already said. You've let people define you to a point but let's not continue down that road. Let God define you."

Looking toward him, she smiles. "That was nice, thank you."

She suddenly stops talking, swiftly bucking her head upwards at the sky. It was so quick and sudden he's caught off guard.

He looks up, "Am I missing something, what do you see?"

"There's a full moon tonight. It's so beautiful."

He agrees and breathes a sigh of relief.

"Do I scare you?" she asks.

"No, you don't scare me," Jack says, smiling.

"I know I'm different, but I'm manageable, *I think*," she says. "I'm very aware of my physical limitations."

"Kelly, everybody is different, some more than others but none are spared, and you're right, it's all in how you feel about them and how they're managed. May that ease your mind."

"I do feel I can be honest with you, Jack."

"I really wish you would. Tell me more about your manageable condition. Tell me what happened last night at the end of our talk?"

"End of our talk?" she echoes, nervously.

"Well, you--"

"Jack, I am so embarrassed because I don't remember acting that way, at all. I really don't."

Jack clears his throat then continues the conversation. Some things have indeed been made clear to him now. "Kelly, can I ask you why you are not on medication? I know your manageable condition has made you feel...well different, but medication could possibly help you."

The face of an angel looks up at him. "I can't, can't, can't... process that word right now." She looks at her shaking hands. "I need to excuse myself. I'm sorry." Smiling as a courtesy, she gets up and heads toward the door. For him, there is a longing to connect with her on a deeper level. He's getting ahead of himself but doesn't know whether to stop now--as her mother warned him to--or to continue to follow his heart.

He feels an urge to connect with her. To him, it's now or never. He gets up and follows her to the living room. "Kelly, wait."

Kelly stops and he reaches for her hands, turning her around to face him. "I know this may sound sudden but..." He gazes into her eyes. "May I kiss you?"

Emma bolts out of the kitchen. "Heck nah, you can't kiss her!"

Kelly jumps back, startled. "I think you better leave now. I think you better leave now. I think you better leave now. I think you better leave now."

Jack reaches for her arms with sternness in his voice, "Stop it!"

With a wide-eyed look of confusion and wonder, she stops. He presses his lips against hers, and she mistakenly bites him.

The blood oozes as he recoils in pain. "You bit me!" he groans but then catches himself. "I mean...I'm sorry."

"No, I am sorry!" Kelly panics and flees to her room, slamming the door shut.

Emma walks past him and opens the front door. "Good night, Mr. Riley."

Licking his wound, he walks out of the house and returns to his car. As he rests his head on the steering wheel, he thinks of his Kelly. What are his intentions? What is he doing here? He's unable to understand, but something keeps driving him toward this woman.

Love is Patient and kind - 1 Corinthians 13:4

CHAPTER 6

KELLY IS IN DEEP THOUGHT locked in her room the next morning. She ponders her fate with Jack Riley, knowing she made a fool of herself again during a stressful moment. *I have never been in such a situation with a man, and it caused me great distress. Will he only think of me now as a slow and truly disturbed woman? What made me think I could handle that?*

"Kelly, are you alright in there?" her mother calls out. "Will you please open the door so we can talk?"

"No, I'm talking to God right now!"

Though Kelly believes that maybe, just maybe, there is a glimmer of hope and light for her prayers; she also knows it cannot possibly be with someone like Jack.

Jack proceeds with his campaign, trying to put Kelly out of his mind but he's not able. When his father asks him what's bothering him, he opens up about Kelly. He tells his family and closest friends about the woman he met and how much he also grew to admire her. He tells them everything and leaves nothing out.

"Yes, she was challenged slightly, but aren't we all?" he asserts. "I think some of it stems from being held back by fear in her own mind."

Jack's father and brother think he is losing his mind and should go no further before real damage is done to all involved. They believe no one can fathom the extent of her disability and where it could lead in the future. His mother is the only one who tells him to pray on it and follow his heart.

Carter invites himself over to his brother's place. On the elevator ride to the fourth floor condo, he ponders his words, hoping that his wisdom can cause a change of heart and encourage Jack to seek love elsewhere. Just for a split second, he lets his finger hover over the down button but Carter realizes he must have this conversation and he must have it now.

Jack's face drops momentarily as he opens the door and sees his brother. "So, what brings you by unannounced?"

"Geez, it's good to see you too, little brother," Carter says.

Jack watches him get comfortable in his favorite red leather lounge chair.

"Man, I gotta get me one of these chairs but anyway, down to business."

"Please, don't." Jack tries to stop him, but Carter presses on, anyway.

"You know, I love you. We look out for each other. We come to the aid of one another. I hope you'll open up and listen to your big bro. I've saved you before."

Jack coughs. *You didn't save me.*

"Brother man, I know you think you can fix everything and everybody with your high ideals and virtues, but this is a whole 'nother ballgame."

Jack crosses his arms and leans against the counter, hoping Carter was done.

Carter lowers his eyes to the floor. "Just hear me out. I am sorry man, she sounds like a beautiful person, outside and inside, but you know exactly what I mean. I know you are a caring and compassionate soul, but I'm wondering if you're taking this a little too much to heart. This is going to take all the patience, love and strength you have. You've got the campaign going on right now. Do you really need a distraction?"

"She's worth it."

"But why does it have to be her?" Carter asks. "You can have any woman you want. You're a good catch and you know it. Remember Marilyn Chavers--

whooaa, now she was something--pursuing that grad in aeronautics! Come to think of it, about the only thing you would give her was the time of day, literally! Jack, have you taken up smokin' something again?"

Jack presses his eyes shut, his head pounding from the rushing adrenaline. "First of all, you are acting like an arrogant snob, and you weren't raised that way." Jack burst out, giving in to his emotions. "Don't you ever bring up my past indiscretions ever again. What God has delivered me from, don't ever taunt me with. We could play the tit-for-tat game, but I will not go there with you. I am surprised at your level of disrespect. Are you implying that she's not good enough? That she can't live fully and be loved? Or is it because I'm in the public eye? They nor you have a right to my private life. Have you always chosen wisely in your life, really? Then how come you're divorced? Seriously, get out of my chair and leave, right now."

"Slim, merely trying to give you a little wisdom. You're too altruistic. I'm outta here, love you man!" Carter retorts.

It's been three weeks and Kelly hasn't heard from Jack, and her family isn't concerned at all. They know it's over. All are relieved that she will never see him again. She tries to hide her sadness as best as she could to move on with her life. Emma persuades their cousin Luella to offer Kelly a secretarial position at a family owned insurance firm. She is delighted and accepts the offer. Emma reasons relatives can keep an eye out to see how she handles the everyday working world. *They could also keep other potential wolves away*, Emma thinks. Though she means well, she clearly can't let it go.

Jack struggles with his thoughts--every other one seems to take him back to his time with Kelly. One lonesome evening away from campaign stress, he begins to think he's losing his mind. The struggle is real. He starts to think of God and Kelly.

How could this stranger who seems a little different, affect me this way, he wonders. *Perhaps it's time for me to spend a bit more time with the one who knows all things, which is what I should have been doing all along.*

He rambles through his closet looking for his Bible. He's feeling ashamed for not having acknowledged God for so long and only turning to him now that there is a problem. He remembers the vow to serve Him. He thanks God for grace then asks for wisdom and life direction.

"God, I need your help with this situation. Why would I be drawn to this woman, and what could I possibly offer her? I humbly ask for your guidance and help right now, Lord!" Flipping open his Bible, it surprises him when the page is opened to Proverbs 31:10. It's the account of the virtuous woman. *What does this mean?* He reads the passage over and over then falls asleep.

While resting, the answer comes to calm his mind. *"Trust in Me. I have prepared you for this."*

He's startled awake and looks around. *Is that you, God? Sorry, I ain't there yet. Was that you?* He hears it again.

"Trust in Me. I have prepared you for this," the voice says.

God's trying to tell me something. Well, I feel better that's for sure.

The following morning, he can't wait to call Kelly.

Tiffy answers the phone, and upon learning who's on the other end, she almost chokes on her breakfast sausage. "Oh, my! Hi, Jack. Kelly is not here, she's at work," Tiffy says almost reluctantly.

"At work, really?" He sounds surprised. "She's putting that degree to work already, I see. That's awesome. I guess I'll call back later, thank you."

Tiffy tells her mother and Jessie about the phone conversation with Jack as Jessie prepares to leave for work. They are all in shock. Emma is still pondering what the man could possibly want. She thought the situation had been taken care of. She tells her daughters not to mention the call to Kelly, for now.

"Do not call her at work," Emma insists. "We will wait to see if he indeed does call back. I need to know what's really on this guy's mind." Emma realizes she needs Godly wisdom and decides to pray for more understanding.

"We should keep telling him she's not here and follow up with something like *we sent her away to live with other relatives.*" Tiffy laughs.

Jessie rolls her eyes. "Tiffy, you're the cleverest woman I know--a real Sherlock—but you just told the man she's at work, and the next time he calls, it's well, she's moved away to live with relatives. Indeed, we need to send you away!"

"It was just a joke. You're too serious, lighten up!" Tiffy teases.

Emma is not interested in their bickering. She's too busy thinking how in the world she's going to get rid of this man, or if she should just let the chips fall where they may. Her mind is playing tricks on her.

What is she so afraid of?

CHAPTER 7

THE SANDERS HOUSEHOLD is unusually quiet this evening. Kelly is home from work, but she's still working on some job projects. Tiffy is watching the evening news on future presidential candidates. *I should run for office* as she snickers. Jessie is going over documents regarding the nursing profession, her secret passion which she hopes to fulfill one day.

"Hey Jessie, if I ran for office you'd be first in line behind momma to vote for me, right?"

Jessie pays her no attention.

Ms. Sanders has taken to her room and is praying. Her door is slightly opened as Kelly walks down the hall. She hears her mother's voice then realizes she's praying. She stops when she hears her own name mentioned.

"Lord, show me what I need to know and how I need to pray in this situation. What are this man's intentions with my daughter? You know his heart, I don't. And neither of us want to see Kelly severely hurt or lose her sanity. Please, show me what's in my heart. Am I just afraid of losing her to someone else because I won't be able to guard her anymore? Could this really turn into something more? After all, I've always been her protector. You know that, Lord."

"No, I have always been her protector, it has been me and not you, only trust me!"

"Yes, Lord."

What is she talking about? There's no relationship. Why is she praying in this manner? Kelly wonders as she leaves the doorway.

The phone rings and Tiffy and Jessie face each other. No one wants to answer. It rings again and, finally, Kelly responds.

"Oh hi, cousin Luella. I'm doing well, yes, I'm working on it now. No, it's not stressing me at all. Okay, see ya tomorrow." Kelly hangs up, chuckling at her cousin's concern.

Once more, Tiffy and Jessie gaze at each other momentarily, this time grinning. The phone immediately rings again, and since Kelly is still by the phone, she picks up. "Hello?"

"Hello, is this Kelly? Hi, this is Jack Riley."

There is a long pause from Kelly. "Uh, yes, hi Jack.

It's nice to hear from you."

"I'm sorry I'm just now getting back to you. All I have been doing besides my campaign work, if you can believe this, is thinking about you. You've made it a little hard for me to keep my focus. So, if you will allow me, I would really like to see you again."

Kelly is overjoyed but too bashful as she's trying to contain her emotions. "Yes, Jack, of course. I would like to see you again, as well."

"Great, I would like to take you out to Swank's tomorrow. I'll pick you up around 7:00 p.m. Hope your mom doesn't mind," he says, amusingly.

"I'm sure it'll be fine," Kelly says with a smile.

Once Kelly hangs up, Tiffy and Jessie are staring at their sister, speechless. Kelly tells them that it was Jack on the phone. "Can you believe it? He wants to take me out to Swanks tomorrow. I'm so nervous, yet so excited."

Grinning, Tiffy chimes, "Oh, how nice Kelly. How nice for you."

"Oh, what is Swank's?" Kelly asks.

"It's just some hole in the wall place," Tiffy says. "You can absolutely wear jeans and a sweatshirt. It's a place where you can relax and be yourself, and that's what you want, right?"

Jessie looks at Tiffy, wondering why she was lying to Kelly. Everyone knows that Swank's is the newest fine dining venue in town. And...there is a dress code.

"Great, okay. As long as I fit in," Kelly says with an

innocent smile. She trusts her sisters.

When Kelly exits, Jessie shakes her head. "You know that's not right."

"Well, you didn't stop me, did you? You're equally at fault," Tiffy says.

"Well, I'm going in there right now to tell her the truth before she embarrasses herself," says Jessie.

"Well, it's too late now. She's going to wonder why we deceived her, and it may upset her for the night. It's done now. It may open up a can of worms," Tiffy says.

"You mean why *you* deceived her, not me. Oh, my Sherlock sister again," says Jessie.

"Let's just see how Jack reacts. This could be a good test for him," says Tiffy.

The next morning, Emma learns of the date night that has been set. She doesn't have much to say and offers only a smile. At work, Kelly can't keep her mind on her task thinking about Jack. Luella notices her seeming preoccupation and asks if she's feeling okay.

"Oh, oh, I'm fine. Did I do something wrong? Was the report okay, you never got back to me on it?"

"The report was an outstanding piece of work, forgive me, I've been so busy today, and I'm just now getting a break. You're doing really well as our secretary, and I want that to continue. If you feel you need some help with anything or are starting to feel overwhelmed, please let me know, okay?"

"Okay. Thank you."

Her uncle Terry stops by to give her a ride home as she is more than eager to get there--to prepare for the night. Emma questions her about the upcoming date. "So, Jack wants to see you again, huh? Is there anything you want to talk to me about before you go out tonight?"

Kelly ponders and says, "No. I'm going to be myself. I'm fine, I think. We'll see how it goes."

"Well, I hope you have a great time tonight. Please pray first and don't be anxious. You're right, be yourself my precious, for that is all you can be. And that is enough!"

"Thanks, Mom." A sudden overwhelming sense of sadness as if from nowhere comes upon her. *Who do I think I'm fooling?* "Do you really think I'm prepared for this? I heard you talking with him, and he still wants to see me."

Not wanting to see her hope diminish, Emma's voice is choking also. "I know you have challenges but you deserve the best and if he isn't the best for you, time will tell. It's time to get out there and explore. What have I been telling you all your life? How does your Father in heaven feel about you? What does He tell you? Don't bring back those old voices of long ago.

Remember, there are no second-class citizens. That phrase is certainly not in God's vocabulary, so you know not to claim it as a part of yours." Wiping her eyes, Emma whispers, "Kelly, my darling, you are a prize that I have been holding on to just a little too tight."

"But what do I have to offer him?" Kelly questions. "I can't even have a child. You know what the doctor said about my insides."

"My dear, he may seem to have everything, but there is obviously something missing. He's not perfect, though from appearances he seems to have it all together. There's something he has not found in any other woman thus far. A woman that has touched his heart. I believe he sees something in you that's worth more than all the education, fine up-bringin', class, money or whatever else you think he has. He knows you're unique and special. If this leads to something more, I believe he could handle it. Besides, don't worry 'bout any of that, right now. You certainly ain't there, yet. Haven't been out with the man and talking 'bout children already."

They both laugh.

"I love you so much, Mom." Kelly wraps her mother in a tight embrace. "I am so blessed to have you in my life. Oh, can you help me with my makeup?"

"Make-up? Watch out now, don't hurt da man! You trying to kill him on the first date?"

Kelly waves her mother off as they both laugh.

Kelly spends the next hour getting ready. Emma asks Tiffy and Jessie what's taking Kelly so long to shower and throw on some jeans. Tiffy is giggling.

It's ten minutes before seven and the doorbell rings. "Wow, he's just a bit early, isn't he?" Tiffy states, amused.

Jessie calls for her youngest sister as Tiffy goes for the door. Jack looks debonair and dashing in his navy suit, sporting beautiful yellow roses. Both women momentarily forget that the man standing before them is not there for the two of them. Jessie rarely shows emotion, but tonight there's a blush. Tiffy's mouth opens wide as she's wondering when her next hair appointment is scheduled. She wants to inquire about some of his friends or relatives but restrains herself.

"You look very nice, and those flowers are beautiful. Can I smell them, Mr. Riley?" asks Tiffy.

Jack is amused. "Why thank you, but I would like Kelly to get first dibs if you don't mind. And please, call me Jack."

"Sure, Mr. Riley. I mean, Jack. I have a question. The gentleman in the restaurant that was talking to us, I think his name is Tony, right?"

"Yes, my young protégé. What about him?"

"Well, is he single and if he is, can you mention me?" asks Tiffy, unashamedly.

Before Jack can answer, Emma walks in. "Hello Jack, it's nice to see you again. You are very handsomely dressed tonight. I would even say a bit overdressed for--"

"Mom, Kelly's here," Tiffy interrupts before Emma can finish her sentence.

Grinning at Jack, Kelly looks down at her own outfit. He is no doubt surprised at her choice of outfit. While she is a beauty to behold, he was hoping to see her in something he had never seen before. A drop dead gorgeous woman in a beautiful dress, grinning in his face as he whisks her away. Instead, he gets a beauty in jeans and a sweatshirt.

The signals must have gotten crossed somehow, but he doesn't dare ask why. *I did say Swank's, I believe.* He's sure someone in the family has something to do with it. Jessie stands back, taking it all in. Jack hears muffled laughter from another room and recognizes it to be Tiffy's voice. He has a feeling but resists the desire to disturb this moment.

"Kelly, you look absolutely ravishing. Here, these are for you."

"Thank you, they're lovely."

 Emma can't help but wonder why they're dressed so differently. Perhaps, they're not compatible after all. "Give me those, sweetheart. You both go on and have a nice time," she says, taking the flowers from Kelly.

"Thanks, Mom."

"Thank you, Mrs. Sanders." Jack flashes Emma a polite smile. "I won't bring her home too late."

As the door shuts, Tiffy comes out of hiding rather tickled.

"What is so funny, lady?" Emma asks, reaching for a vase on the shelf. "Isn't it beautiful that your baby sister's going out on a date with a wonderful gentleman?"

As Tiffy continues to laugh, Emma demands to know what is tickling her so. Jessie, rolling her eyes as a hint to stop, yields no results. Tiffy spills the beans without mercy as if she gets great enjoyment from her words.

Emma is not pleased. She stands tall and erect as never before with both hands on her hips. She does not hold back. "What in the world have I raised here? Have you lost your cotton-picking mind? Do you have any idea, any, of what your sister is going through? Obviously, you do, 'cause you've been raised with her. You've always come through for her, so what in Sam's name has gotten ahold of you, Tiffy? What were you thinking? Jessie, did you know about this?"

Jessie starts to open her mouth, but her mother keeps shouting, her attention still on Tiffy. "Am I dealing with a kindergartener, here? Put yo' self in her shoes. That was deceitful!"

Tiffy sinks into the couch.

"When was the last time you two had a date?" Emma goes on. "All my children are good-looking and have character. I didn't raise y'all any other way. You three always stick together. If something is meant to become of this, it will happen. If not, then it won't. I know it seems far-fetched to you, but it's not your job to put a damper on it. Do I sense a little unwarranted jealousy going on here? I am so angry and disappointed right now."

Tiffy's voice cracks in a whisper, "You know what, actually, I am feeling a little jealous. Kelly has gotten a lot of attention through the years. The focus, it seems, has always been on her. Kelly this, Kelly that, watch out for Kelly. Let's try to keep her motivated and sane. Let's help her get through. Ummm, let's protect and defend her. Well, what about me? It's like...it's been all about *her* happiness."

Emma doesn't respond. She's not quite sure what to say.

Sniffling, Tiffy continues, "Yes, I am a grown woman but most times I feel as if I can't leave this house. I have to stick around to keep an eye on her – sort to speak. And Jessie, deep down you know you feel the same way. You just hold everything in."

Jessie turns her head away from them both.

"Inwardly Momma, I really, really don't believe you want us to leave," Tiffy adds. "You've gotten so used to this arrangement."

Emma closes her eyes. She knows there is some truth in what her daughter is saying. Spreading her eagle arms around them both, the weeping starts.

"I... hmm..." Emma can hardly speak through her tears. "Please, please forgive your momma. Please forgive me for not seeing what I should have seen, for tossing the clues to the side. I realize I've sheltered all of my daughters and we're all due for a change, not just Kelly. You know, I do believe there's a purpose in what is happening in Kelly's life, and it's the start of some needed healing in all of us. This has brought out true feelings and things that needed to be spoken outright, and for that, well, I thank you, Tiffy. I am so glad you were honest. You're right. I guess, I always thought things would be the same though I prayed for change. That was not right."

The girls cry in their mother's arms.

"Please, believe me. It was never my intention to hold you two back from anything you've ever wanted in life. I wanted good things for all my beautiful daughters. If you felt that you've been tied here because of Kelly, then please forgive me for putting that extra burden on you. You did not deserve that. I always thought what happened to your sister was in some way my fault, and I had to make up for it. I'm sorry that I unconsciously made all three of us pay. I've been so wrong, so so wrong, but you are a grown woman. You've always been free to pursue your own goals. I apologize if I gave you the impression that you needed my permission to somehow move on," Emma laments.

They all tighten their arms around each other.

"But what you did was still wrong, Tiffy." Emma looks at her daughter with disapproving eyes. "You should've never deceived your sister."

"You're right, and I'm sorry," Tiffy says.

"I'm so glad we had this talk," Jessie smiles. "And I feel just so happy. We're gonna be fine."

"Me too." Tiffy smiles. "In fact, I've decided to pursue that degree at Jackson State in Speech Communications finally. I will continue to work part-time. I'm good at running my mouth as you all know!"

They all laugh.

"And as for me," Jessie chimes, "I've been inspired to go after that two year nursing degree I've been dreaming about. I feel the time is right, and in a sense, Kelly has led the way. And for the record, I'm not worried about a man right now! If you allow me to stay here until I finish, I promise I'm outta here to Chicago."

"Of course, sweetheart."

"Wow, who would have thought it. We helped our baby sis, and now she's helping us and doesn't even realize it. What you give out, does come back, doesn't it? In unusual ways sometimes," Jessie adds.

"Well said, sweetheart." Emma kisses both of her girls on their foreheads. "I'm very grateful and happy tonight, ladies. This has been some evening. I need to take a seat. God is in the plans. It's never too late."

CHAPTER 8

"JACK, YOU LOOK very attractive," Kelly says as Jack opens the car door for her. "I thought we were going to a casual place?"

"We are," Jack says, not wanting her to feel bad. "I just thought you said you wanted me to wear a suit, tonight."

"I never said that, but it's nice to see you in it." Kelly smiles, though still feeling a bit embarrassed. "I'm sorry, I'm dressed so..."

"You look beautiful." He leans in for a kiss but stops, "Don't you bite me."

They both laugh.

"No kisses please, the opening attempt the other day was a mistake, don't you think?"

No, not really but "Okay, sorry," he says.

Jack ditches the dinner jacket and takes her to a place where she would feel more comfortable. After placing their order at *Maurice's café,* they sit outside to enjoy the beautiful balmy weather.

"Your mother is very protective of you," Jack says. "How does that make you feel? Do you sometimes feel hemmed in?"

"Wow, so many questions on that but you know what, I'm so used to it. She's my mother, so I guess she'll never stop looking out for me, even if she goes overboard at times. I'm assuming that's how your mother feels, as well."

"Yes, but there is a difference..." He stops himself. "You know what, we'll talk about that some other time. How about we get to know more about each other?"

"Like-like what?"

"Where is your father?"

"He passed away many years ago and went to heaven."

Jack pauses, "Wow, so sorry. How did he get there so early?"

"Through Jesus, of course."

Jack smiles. "I hope to meet him one day."

"He died in a car accident when I was just a tot," Kelly goes on. "I don't remember him, but my mother often told me he was an attentive father and husband who loved us so very much. I often wonder why God took him so young. A father's love is always needed."

"I am so sorry that happened to your father, and so soon. Sounds like a great man who had a lot more living to do. And I don't proclaim to know all the answers, but I do know that God did not do that to your father. He didn't will it. It was allowed, and I don't pretend to know why. But as the scripture says, *Now we see things imperfectly, like puzzling reflections in a mirror, but then we will see everything with perfect clarity.* We may not understand it all right now but one day we will."

She studies him for a second, knowing what he is saying is true, then offers him a smile. "My mother told me my father was her one true love. He had gone to Chicago about a job offer and stayed a couple of days extra to visit relatives. It was the dead of winter, and my mom was uneasy about him traveling at that time. The 15th of January of '79, a day to remember for us. Every time she would tell us the story, it was verbatim so we wouldn't forget any detail of that fateful winter. She wanted us to remember that Charles Sanders passed away trying to give his family a better life."

"Will you tell it to me?" Jack asks.

"If you want me to."

"I do."

"*Charles, wait at least 'till March. You know how Chicago is this time of year, please,*" Momma pleaded.

"*Look, ain't no money to fly, and the man said if I*

could get there and check out the area and proposal, he could almost guarantee me the job," Dad stressed.

"The man said, the man said--oh phooey! The man ain't driving, you are!" Momma told him.

"Oh, come give me a kiss. You know you want me to move this family to Cheekago!" Dad said as he laughed. "Didn't you wanna leave Jackson? My sister Pearl would love to see them gurls all the time!"

Jack chuckles as Kelly continues the story.

Momma hugged him. "It's -those girls- Charles, it's pronounced, -those girls."

Jack gets a kick out of that line.

"You know they don't talk like that in Cheekago," Momma told him.

"Dad made it to Chicago and was returning with good news. He told his boss he was ready to start a new life and inquired about the housing market. My Aunt Pearl told us dad was so excited about receiving the offer that he couldn't wait to come back home. He was warned about the weather and to listen to the reports before taking that long drive back to Jackson, but he shrugged it off."

"It wasn't the pretty white crisp snow or the blinding torrential rain, but instead, it was the stinking monstrous fog that took my daddy's life. Traffic had slowed to a crawl. The semi-truck driver behind him didn't see his vehicle until it was too late. He just couldn't stop in time as it barreled into the back of Dad's pickup. All the driver said was that he heard screeching metal and the sound of impact before blacking out. Not only was he driving too fast but he was drunk. As soon as we heard, my mother became sick and had to be hospitalized. She often told us if it had not been for us--her children--she would have lost her mind. It was prayer that sustained and pulled us all through."

Jack wipes tears from Kelly's eyes.

"I'm sorry, didn't mean to put a damper on our conversation." Kelly apologizes. "It's just that I've never had the opportunity to share with anyone--outside of my family--what happened to my father."

"It's perfectly fine." Jack gazes into her eyes. "I'm glad you felt comfortable enough to share. I like that. That was pretty rough on you all, but as you said, you made it through by God's grace."

"Thank you, but I would really like to change the subject now, please."

"Yes, ma'am. So, what do you like to do in your spare time?"

"Well, I read a lot, mostly classics. Not a big fan of romance--I gave up on those. My sisters and I hang out a lot, going here and there when we're free. I'm working now, so that is taking up more of my time, before it was school. I've never been out of Jackson, but I would sure love to travel and see the world. I would love that."

"Wow, wow, you've never been out of Jackson?" Jack asks, unable to mask his surprise.

A puckered brow appears as she glares at him.

"I mean, you've never had the pleasure of leaving this lovely town to see another lovely town?"

They both snicker.

"No, I haven't, but I've got relatives in Chicago and Florida. We've never actually visited them, though. They always come here."

"Well, we'll have to see what we can do about that," Jacks says with a smile. "You're missing a lot!"

"So, what's your story?" Kelly asks. "What keeps you here, besides the requirements of your job?"

"You do."

She lowers her head, shyly. "You just met me. That's not a good enough reason. Could it be that you want to make a contribution to the city you were born and raised in?" she asks.

"Sure I do, but I had planned on leaving at some point," Jack confesses. "So, you may be reason enough to keep me here. You're a special lady, Kelly."

"Jack, that is sweet but there are a lot of pretty, unassuming, and certainly more intelligent, women out there than me."

"Perhaps, but none of them interests me. Why is that so hard to believe?" he asks, still holding her gaze.

"Because you're a good looking and extremely intelligent public figure," she says. "I don't fit the standard mold of who you should be pursuing. I'm not Ivy League. I get lost at times and... well, you know what I mean."

"Don't put me on a pedestal. I don't belong there," Jack says. "And if you don't want to take this any further because you feel we can't add value to each other's lives, then let me know right now. I'll walk away."

Her eyes buck wide. She wasn't expecting that comment. Swallowing hard, Kelly turns her head away, not knowing what to say. *He's giving me a way out. Should I take it? Or should I face my fears and see where this goes?*

"If I may be honest..." Jack breaks the silence. "It would be very hard for me to walk away and I think it would be for you, too."

Looking up into his gorgeous light brown eyes, she beams in agreement. "Why don't we talk about something else?"

Jack smiles. "If you'd like."

The couple spend the evening talking about Jack's life as a government official. Though they are far apart in experience, the laughter comes easily as he entertains her with the sometimes funny and strange world of politics. She is beginning to experience feelings she's never felt before. *This has got to be a dream. He's so sweet, easy-going and understanding. How long have you known this man? Guard your heart, girl!*

"Kelly, let me tell you a little story about someone I used to know, and why I do what I do." Jack pauses as he waits for the waiter to bring them their order. "So, I took a ride down to Chuck Daddy's bar late one evening. I used to hang out with some local young guys during my run for alderman. I would shoot ball with them and talk to them about life and turning the tide. On this particular night, I scanned the neighborhood, looking for a familiar face. I lamented that nothing had changed."

Kelly leans in, listening attentively.

"There they were across the street in the park, Sammy Olsen and his friends. I tried many times to get through to those kids--especially Sammy. He was about seventeen and pretty savvy, too savvy. I ventured to try one more time, especially on that night. I asked him where he saw himself in ten years..."

"How should I know man, I mean sir?" The sarcasm was evident as he bowed down in front of me. He and his gang were living in so much dysfunction it was all they knew or believed there was."

"I haven't always lived a clean life. Do you want to hear my story?" I asked.

"Not really," he said.

Kelly giggles and Jack smiles.

"Well, fine, but I'd like to tell you what I see in you if you start thinking differently."

"Awe man, I don't want to hear that same ol', same ol' tired bull that we all done heard before!" Sammy remarked.

"Can I at least give you my vision for a second?" I

asked.

Sammy said, "Alright, whatever," as he turned his back.

"I see you finishing school or getting that GED, against the odds, against the environment, and against the naysayers. Sticking with it, not only for your future and your future family. They will see that it can be done and perhaps someone will be inspired because you moved first. It simply takes one to break away from the tide and pull others in. Give them and us somethin' good to talk about. You've got it in you. When you conquer that one thing, you will be so inspired, I already know it. Others will be watching you 'cause you are a leader. You are leading a gang right now which means you know how to influence people. What if you could turn that around for the good of your community? After getting that diploma, your next step could possibly be a higher education."

"You got dreams hiding in you. You can talk to me about 'em. I believe in you. Now, you've got to believe in yourself and not the negative mess somebody else told you. You're standing in your own way, listening to those voices. Think about the family you want to have someday. Huh, you know, I can even see you becoming a doctor."

"A doctor, a doctor," shouted Luther, the second in command, as they all howled with laughter. "Whew, that was a good one, that was good, what else you got, man?"

"I told Luther he was my other little bro from another planet, and I saw him becoming a nurse, and to another, I told him he could wipe butts as an aide. They all fell out again with laughter as I tickled myself."

Kelly laughs. "Did you think wiping butts would impress them toward change?" she asks.

"Well, of course not, but I told them not to laugh 'cause it's noble, and somebody has to do it. Heck, I might need mine wiped one day. It pays bills and supports families and keeps us off the streets. Then I did it. I promised Sammy a job working with me if I was elected to office. I gave him my contact information and told him he could call me anytime."

"That was very nice of you," Kelly says.

"Sammy stopped and stared at me as if he was thinking, this man is serious and I just may follow through. I repeated that I believed in him and I wanted to help him change his life. As he continued to stare, Luther grabbed him by the arm and pulled him away from me. That was the last time I saw him. I was hoping to hear from him, but..." Jack pauses. "He was killed two weeks later. He wanted out of the gang. That, that hurt me big time. I felt I was getting through, but then I lamented that maybe I could have handled it better. A life I thought I was influencing, got away. The look on Sammy's face walking away haunts me to this day. I know I had him, I just know it. He wanted out." Jack pauses. "But Kelly, the fight's not over."

Her hands are covering her mouth as a tear rolls down her cheek. "That is awful, just awful. I can only imagine how much that hurt you but like you said, the fight's not over. There are thousands of Sammy's out there, looking for guidance and leadership. I am so proud of you, Jack."

Beaming, Jack reaches for Kelly's hand. "Thanks, I really needed to hear that."

"Boy, we've managed to laugh and cry all in one night!" Jack says. "Let me get you home before your mom kills me."

Kelly giggles like a young school girl.

CHAPTER 9

A FTER A TIRING DAY of late evening work, Kelly's cousin Luella drops her off at home. A lovely arrangement of yellow roses sits atop a package in her living room. *Wow, who are those for?*

Tiffy walks in eating a baloney sandwich and mumbling, "Yeah that's for you Kelly. Want a bite?"

Kelly takes in a whiff of the delicately fragrant flowers. *Oh yeah, I needed this.* Jack's work has kept him away from Kelly for nearly two weeks. *Okay, he's just busy girl you can breathe now.* She takes the items to her room.

Suddenly, her bedroom door flies open and Tiffy walks in.

"Hey, what you got there?" Tiffy asks. "Been

waiting for you to get home so I can get a peek, too."

"Wow, I can't get any privacy around here, especially lately."

"Sorry sis, I'm just as excited as you are." Tiffy peeks into the box. "So, what is it?"

"It's a collection of books," Kelly says, a wide smile growing on her face. "The first two are Politics 101 and 102. I think he's trying to teach me something."

They both let out a hearty laugh. "Looks like the next ones are... *Breaking out of Your Comfort Zone* and *God said I Love You as You Are.*"

"Awww," bellows Tiffy. "Wait, there's more?"

"*Sense & Sensibility* and the remaining two are on traveling for fun. I'm not going to explain the significance of the titles to you, Tiff."

Tiffy stares at her sister. "Okay," *but it's pretty obvious, Kelly.* Reaching her hand into the bottom of the box, "Oh look, here's a note at the bottom." Tiffy grabs it.

"Dear Kelly, if you are reading this..."

Kelly snatches the note back and asks her sister to leave the room.

"Okay, I get it." Tiffy throws her arms in the air. "Notes are private."

"Dear Kelly, if you are reading this, you must have taken all the books out and have now reached the bottom of the box, that's good. It means you were interested in the whole content of the box. You didn't stop when you saw Politics 101. I like that. By the way, glad you gave up reading romance novels. I would not have known where to start with those. And besides, you don't need them anymore, you can read me. I am romance."

Whooaa, my legs are feeling weak. I need to sit down. Never felt this way before. It's a nice feeling, though. I'm not sure of this. This is much too fast. Guard your heart girl, don't lose it! "Maaaaaaaa," she shouts, laughing to herself. "What is happening to me?" *Oh boy, I better read the politics' books first.*

Their relationship blossoms at full speed ahead. Spending more time together--as his schedule allows--has brought them much closer. He has begun to understand her quirks and fears, and they find they have more in common than not. They are falling in love despite the continued skepticism of some family and friends. They've prayed together and they've prayed apart. His patience and understanding are paying off. Along the journey, he's taught her many things about life in areas where a little time and inspiration were needed.

On a quiet evening after dinner, Jack invites Kelly shopping.

"Hey, how about we take a ride and then do a little

shopping? I need to pick up a few dress shirts. You can help me, and then we can find a nice little boutique on Grand Boulevard. In fact, a new one *Class with Sass* just opened. I'm sure we can find some items you would look great in. With that slim figure, you would look great in a nice dress and heels. I'm picturing the color peach against your beautiful skin and lovely brown hair. That's one of my favorite colors."

Kelly's confidence took a little hit. "Oh, is there something wrong with the way I dress? You've never complained before, why now? I've never been fashion conscious. Besides, I don't buy designer clothes. My family is not rich like yours."

"Wow, I'm sorry. I was in no way referencing your financial status, but just so we're clear, I didn't carry a silver spoon in my mouth growing up. My dad worked his butt off in odd jobs to make life better for us. We wore the same pair of jeans for 5 days of school and would wear the next pair the following week. I got teased a lot. So, I know what both sides feel like."

Kelly lowers her head as Jack goes on.

"I want to give you what I have and dress you like the queen that you are. God doesn't mind us owning things as long as those things don't own us. We're the King's kids, and he blesses us so we can be a blessing to others." Jack lifts her chin and looks into her eyes. "Kelly, I want to be a blessing to you."

"Why?" Kelly asks.

'Cause I, I, well, I love you."

She's fighting back the tears as he embraces her. *This is the first time he has said that to me.* "I lo-ove, ove you, too."

A simple kiss lingers and they both become emotional, wanting their passions to take over. But fighting against all fleshly desires, Jack backs off.

"Hmm, I think we need to leave my condo and get you home, right away. We'll just postpone our shopping for some other time," he says.

"Yeah, good idea," Kelly agrees. "Can I just say something before we leave?"

"Sure."

"I just want to say that I believe in you, and I thank you for believing in me. My earlier reaction was just an old fear of not being accepted for who I am, but I am open to more change. It's like what God does, he accepts us first as we are in all our mess, then change soon follows."

"That's right." Jack smiles. "Kelly, you are the bravest woman I know, and truth is, even if you want to wear sackcloth, I won't stop you. You look beautiful in anything."

Kelly blushes, and Jack presses his lips to her forehead.

Often in their fun times, they enjoy one of her favorite

activities—dancing to classic soul music. It takes some convincing to get Jack off the couch. He knows he had inherited two left feet.

"Mr. Politician, you are a wee too serious." Kelly teases as she stands at the center of her living room "So, what if dancing is the only thing you can't do! Don't ever lose the child in you. Never forget how to laugh and keep your song."

"Okay, okay. I'll keep trying but only if you go sailing or rock climbing with me," Jack muses. "You've got to be a little more adventurous, too."

"Are you calling dancing adventurous?" She laughs, and he surrenders. She brings out the kid in him, and he brings out more of the adult in her. "Jack do you think you could introduce Tony to my sister?" she asks as she dances in his arms to *Reach Out, I'll be There.*

"Which sister?" He widens his eyes, and Kelly laughs.

"My sister is a nice person, she really is."

"Do you want to know what I think?" Jack spins her around then pulls her close. "I know that, and I don't want to step out of bounds with my opinions, but I really don't think she's ready. I think there's some soul searching needed and when she is ready, the right one will find her. "

I wonder if he's saying that I'm the right one for him. There's something else I need to tell him about me. It's not written in stone where this is going. Maybe I may not have to tell him. I'll wait just a little longer.

"Besides, Tony's got too many women. He's not ready for a real relationship."

"What about your brother?"

Jack almost chokes on his own spit. "Kell, come on now. You can't be serious."

"Why not?"

"She couldn't handle my brother—and vice versa. Butting heads is no way to start a relationship. You would hate me later."

Kelly nodded, he had a point. "Just wanted you to choke on your spit is all."

"That was mean," he says.

They both laugh.

Kelly is finally invited to dinner to meet Jack's family--his parents and his brother.

"You're different," Jack's mother points out as she finishes her tea. "I can't wait to finally meet the woman who has had a hand in that. What I don't understand, however, is what took so long?"

"I just wanted to be sure of a few things first. Now, please behave tonight. She means a lot to me."

The Riley's live in one of Jackson's wealthiest communities, Heatherton Estates.

"My parents are really nice and down to earth, Kelly. I'm sure they will like you. Just be yourself, and if you feel a little nervous, it's alright. I'll be right there with you."

Jack's parents' house is everything Kelly thought it would be. She admires the beauty as they enter the circular driveway to the huge two story colonial. *She's driven by this area before but never thought she'd be graced to walk inside one of these homes.* The yellow striped awnings stand out against the white brick. Red tulips line the path to the double front door. The grassy area is vast, meticulous and expertly manicured.

Entering the palatial home, she is met with intense stares from Jack's father, Antonio. He's trying to understand if the physical bears any resemblance to what he's heard about her. Well, she certainly is beautiful, he couldn't deny that. Reminds him of Laurie when she was younger with all that curly hair.

"Mom, Dad. I would like you to meet Kelly Sanders. Kelly, these are my parents--Antonio and Laurie Riley."

"It's a pleasure to meet you." Kelly extends her hand.

"The pleasure is all ours," says Laurie, taking Kelly's hand. "You are so lovely, my dear. I have been waiting to meet you. Won't you please take a seat and get comfortable?"

"Oh and this is my brother, Carter!" Jack

announces as Carter walks in.

"Hi ya doing?" Carter says.

"I'm well, thank you." Kelly takes note of the vintage-inspired living room with dark brown carpeting and long tan paisley sofa. *At least the walls are white.* Beautiful old oil paintings are on one wall next to family memorabilia. She takes it all in and wonders how she will decorate her own home someday, something she never really thought about before. "You have such a lovely home," she comments to Laurie.

"Why, thank you, dear!"

Kelly could sense she was being scrutinized by Carter, as well. Trying to play on her uneasiness, he stares as if she were queer. "So Kelly, what degree did you earn online?" asks Carter.

"I, I, I, I...." She looks over at Jack's smiling face. "I earned it in Liberal Arts."

Antonio looks down as Laurie smiles.

"Why, that's great!" Carter cheers. "What do you plan on doing with your degree?"

"I, I haven't decided yet," she answers.

"You know Jack has a master's in Public Policy and he was talking about going for the doctorate. He just needs to use his time more wisely."

She stares at him for a moment. *More wisely? What does he mean by that?* "That would be great, not only is he very intelligent but he's graced with people skills and a lot of wisdom which I admire even more."

"What do you think of our presidential candidates, this time around?" Carter asks. "Whose platform interests you the most and do you think the tax code needs revising?"

Kelly lowers her head, feeling slightly embarrassed.

"That's enough, Carter." Jack cuts in. "How about you and me step aside for a minute." He turns to Kelly touching the hollow of her back as he whispers,

"Are you alright?"

Kelly nods.

"Are you sure, dear? I must apologize for my son's behavior," Laurie says.

"No, he's a grown man. Let him apologize for himself." Jack turns to face Carter, fuming. "If you think I'm going to just sit here and let--"

"Jack, please." Kelly touches his arm.

"I'm sorry, Kelly. I hope I didn't offend you," Carter says. "It's been a rough day at the office."

"Please accept our sincerest apology, my dear. We don't act like that in this family?" Antonio finally speaks up. "Please, let us be seated for a fabulous dinner as we make sure to include grace first."

The following week, on their usual Thursday evening

get-togethers, Kelly waits for Jack to arrive. She's headed to his home to indulge in one of the special culinary confections he's created.

"Kelly, dear." Emma enters Kelly's room. "You two are on a whirlwind, where is he taking you tonight?"

"His house."

"Careful now, be wise," chimes Emma.

"Yeah, don't bring home no baby," Tiffy teases as she walks by.

Kelly stops dead in her tracks. Her hand freezes on the button of her blouse. As soon as those words left Tiffy's mouth, she knew she had misspoken again.

"Oh, my. I'm so sorry, Kelly. I don't know why I can't keep my mouth in check. I should have been born with a foot in it. Sister, please forgive your birdbrained sister. I love you."

Emma shuts the door, leaving Tiffy outside. "Honey, I think it's time to have the talk with Jack. You're in love with him, and I can see he feels the same. Don't wait any longer, please. He deserves to know."

Kelly slowly gets into Jack's car as if she's in a trance. Wanting to clear the air quickly. "Hey, where's my big grin when you see me?"

"You look lovely, got all that hair pulled back in a ponytail. I like that."

"Thank you," Kelly says, staring out the window.

"Is everything okay?" Jack reaches for her hand.

Looking straight ahead, she hesitates to respond at

first. "Well, there, there, there's something I, I need to tell you and it's really, really important. *Tell him. Don't wait any longer. Tell him.* She hears her mother's voice in her head.

Oh my, she's stuttering, something's up, he's thinking.

"Cou, cou, you pl pl pleeeasee pull over."

"Hmmm...okay." He tries to smile, but it doesn't do much to settle his nerves. "What is it?"

"I, I can't bring myself to say it. I, I, I have just been so happy I, I, I kind of put this subject in the back of my mind but I can't avoid it any longer. Please, forgive me. Please, forgive me."

His heart beats faster with each passing second. "What in the world are you trying to tell me. Look at me, what are you keeping from me?"

"I...I can't, I can't have children!"

After a long silence, Jack finally speaks. "You can't... have children?"

"Jack, I'm so sorry."

"Tell me why, Kelly. Why can't you have children?"

"I, I'm not sure, Jack. I, d-d-don't remember."

"Well, I need you to remember."

"I can't think right now. I n-n-need a minute to process my thoughts."

"Kelly--"

"You're pressuring me, stop it." Kelly starts to cry.

He stares at her. *I'm pressuring you?* "Why would you keep something like that from me?"

She's crying hysterically now, and Jack pulls her into his arms.

The words of what the doctor told her slowly leaks from her mouth. To Jack, it seems like an eternity for her to finish the prognosis. When she finishes, she can't even remember what she said.

"Look, I'm sorry, but disappointment can't even begin to describe how I'm feeling right about now," Jack says with an even longer silence this time. "I think the most heartbreaking of all is you couldn't trust me enough to talk about this before now."

Kelly moves from his grasp. Solemnly speaking, "I was afraid this dream would end as soon as I told you. I ha-have so m-m-many issues, and I didn't want to add to the list. They say what you fear comes upon you. I'm, ugh, ugh am truly sorry. Can you please f-f-find it in your heart to forgive me?"

Closing his eyes, he sighs. "This is going to take some time to process. You don't keep something like that from someone you love. We trust each other, remember? I've got some busy days ahead, and I need time away but..." He looks into her eyes. "Rest assured, I have not changed my mind about our relationship. I just have to process this."

This is disappointing, to say the least, but I do love her.

She's relieved but heartsick at the same time. She knows where she hopes the relationship will go. She heard what he said about not changing his mind. Only time will tell if those words are indeed true.

"Can you just take me back home?" Kelly asks, her voice soft. "I would like to be alone right now."

"Yeah, I think I would too."

Upon Kelly's return so early, Emma looks at her daughter's swollen red face and follows her to her room. She has a pretty good idea of what happened.

"Talk to me, dear. Is everything alright?"

"Oh, Momma. Do you want to know every single detail of my life and conversations? You can't help me with this one. You can't give me the ability to have a child."

"No, I can't, but God can. And like I told you before, if he's the one and he truly loves you, he will accept everything about you. If he doesn't, it'll be okay. It will be alright. You are stronger now than you've ever been. That is a blessing in itself. You know that. I'll say no more. Goodnight."

Kelly's disheartened soul tosses through the night, feeling her dream is ending. *Another thorn in the flesh to live with.* Unable to sleep--and with minimal strength to pray--she sits in bed, thinking. *Maybe I should go back to school or move to Chicago. Maybe I should have revealed this matter to Jack on our first date, then I would have saved myself from all this torture.* A lonely teardrop slowly trickles from her left eye, past her cheek, around her nostril, and into her mouth. Kelly buries her face in her pillow, and a steady stream from both eyes soon follow.

Jack also cannot make the sleep come. Why didn't she tell me? I know it would not have been easy to talk about it but... He hears a still small voice within.

My son, is your love for her based on her ability to give you a child? Are you more concerned about your mother's longing or your love for Kelly? Jack's thoughts divert to his spirit within. *Okay, Lord, I hear you. I need to stop thinking about myself; I love her, regardless.*

Jack desires to reassure Kelly of his love, understanding the pain she feels. Many times throughout the night, he calls her but hangs up before the last digit.

This is not working. Get your behind out of this bed and go see her now. Not caring that it's 3:00am in the morning, he throws on jeans and a t-shirt. The bait's been tossed; he happily reaches for it, and the reel pulls him in. He knows there's no turning back nor indeed does he want to. *I can't.*

On the short drive to London Town, he takes in the empty, silent streets as if they know he needs peace at that moment. Kelly hears a car pull up in front of her home then moments later, the bell rings. She sits up and sees Tiffy head toward the door, rubbing her eyes.

"Jack?" Tiffy says, surprised. "What are you doing here? It's three in the mornin'? And you don't look so good, brother."

Shaking his head in disbelief, he motions to her to keep her voice down. "I'm sorry, I know what time it is, but I need to see your sister."

Kelly appears at the door, and Tiffy steps back. He stares at Kelly with eyes unblinking and for a long time neither says a word. Reaching for her, pulling her toward him, his tall frame squeezes her securely. He does not want to let go. Their lips meet. Peeking into the living room with a head full of rollers, Emma grins from ear to ear while Tiffy playfully covers her eyes.

"All is well," Jack tells Kelly. She feels at peace again, and so does he. "We'll work this out with God's help."

"Amen."

Wow, what am I doing wrong, Tiffy's thinking. *This man ain't real.*

CHAPTER 10

JACK'S MOTHER HAS taken to Kelly and has expressed an interest in helping her. Jack has often spoken to Kelly of his love for his mother's famous stew. Laurie's offer of assistance with the recipe is heartily accepted.

"You have a dream kitchen," Kelly says. "I'm sure you have no problem loving the art of cooking in here. Your stove can make about three of mine. The shiny black counters paired with white cabinets are gorgeous. I like this a lot and with yellow curtains, real nice."

"Kelly, I'm going to let you in on a little secret," Laurie says. "I think it's a bit ostentatious myself. In fact, my husband chose this house. I think it's too big, but I don't tell him that."

The ladies' laughter fills the atmosphere.

"Yes, this recipe may indeed come in handy. Try it soon. It probably won't taste as good as mine, but it may come in an extremely close second."

Kelly snickers. "Will it pass the Jack test?"

"It'll pass."

"Then that's good enough for me."

"Just watch closely and take notes about the number of dashes and pinches."

They both let out another hearty laugh.

I really like her, Laurie thinks to herself.

Antonio is still not convinced about the compatibility of his son and Kelly. Later that day while relaxing in his backyard, he expresses his concerns to his wife. Jack is paying a surprise visit to see his parents before heading to the gym. Hearing snickers from a distance; he decides to come thru the back way. Walking along the side path, his athletic shoes are barely audible. His parents' words become more apparent as he nears the yard. When he hears Kelly's name and *relationship*, he stops and steps behind a bush to listen.

"Where do you think this relationship is headed?" Antonio asks his wife. "I, uh, I mean, I really don't think she's the one for him. They would sure give us beautiful grandchildren, but it's just not a match made in heaven." He pauses before letting out a long heavy sigh. "You know you feel the same way I do, and I've been waiting for you to say it, why won't you say it?"

Jack lowers his head to his chest, the disappointment eating him up inside.

"Honey, why can't you believe he really loves this woman despite what you see as incapabilities?" Laurie picks up the conversation. "This is between your son, Kelly, and the Lord. Take it to the Lord; you are a praying man. Why are you asking me these questions? Do you doubt your son and what you've instilled in him? Let me ask you something--and we've talked about this many, many times before. Remember telling me how being in that chair makes you feel limited? You see yourself differently, and yet you want to be accepted and made to feel that you're no different than anyone else. Those were your words Antonio, and I think they're probably Kelly's as well."

He bows his head without saying a word.

"What I do know is he's our son, and whatever happens we need to support him. I have a peace about it. I like her. Sometimes we don't understand what God is up to. Still, we have to be silent and watch what comes out of our mouths. That's all I have to say about it," Laurie remarks.

Jack has heard enough as he quietly backs away from the house and enters the front door with a key. He is glad his mother is defending him, but his father's words--though he understood his concerns--are still disheartening.

Jack has occasionally taken Kelly on outings to meet some of his colleagues--and to get her used to being in the public eye. Slowly exposing Kelly to his lifestyle has proved beneficial. She has become even more outgoing and engaging and seems to be doing well in public encounters, with his help. In studying up on some of the issues he faces, she has had a way of surprising him with her comprehension of the knowledge.

His closest friends are aware of the unusual circumstances, and though some do not agree, they respect his choices and offer the utmost respect toward Kelly. On a night out at Swank's, Jack and Kelly are having dinner with his best friend and colleague, Robert Foster and his wife, Nina. The conversation is lighthearted and centered on Robert's weight gain.

"I'm trying to knock the jelly but you've got me working hard man, trying to get the word out for you," Robert says to Jack with amusement.

"What are you doing to my husband?" Nina chimes in. "We all want Hester out but these speeches, late nights with snacks to boot are messing with my man's physique."

They all laugh around the table.

"How do you stay in such good shape, Jack?" Nina asks.

"Well, my love has me using my two left feet more

than I've ever used them before." Jack smiles at Kelly. "You know I thought it was impossible to do that, but she's pretty darn smart."

Kelly nudges him playfully and they all chuckle.

She's about to indulge in a dinner of creamy lobster bisque soup, spinach salad and prime rib. "Honey, I can't eat this," Kelly whispers to Jack. "I don't eat seafood, and I can't eat walnuts."

"Excuse me, what did you say?" Jack asks.

"I don't eat this kind of food," she repeats.

"Sweetie," he says softly. "This is the exact same meal you enjoyed at my parent's home with no problem. You told me you really enjoyed it."

Robert and Nina look her way momentarily, then look at Jack. Feeling their eyes on him, he smiles embarrassingly.

"Jack, just order her something else," Nina chimes in.

Scratching his head, he says, "Absolutely, I will do just that."

"She's probably feeling a little tired, right Kelly?" asks Nina.

"Yes, can you order it as a take-out for me?"

"Take out?" Jack echoes.

"I'm sorry," Kelly says.

"No, no. Don't be sorry," Nina tells her.

"It's been a great evening with the two of you," Robert says. "Hopefully there will be many more."

On their way out, Alexandria Mitchell, an assistant

to another colleague at the office is entering the restaurant. There is a male friend with her. She's an attractive, red-haired woman, always strikingly dressed. Her cunning and sharp reputation precedes her. It is the mindset that works best in her male-dominated office, or so she thinks. The staff strains to ignore her behavior due to her skill at negotiation and persuasion being second to none.

"Well, look who's here!" Alexandria greets cheerfully. "Hi, Jack. It's so nice to see you this evening. Hi, Robert...Nina!"

"Alex, let me introduce you to Ms. Kelly Sanders. Kelly, this is Alex. She works as an assistant at the office."

"Hello, Alex. That's a nice outfit."

"It's Alexandria. And thank you. I buy all my suits at Bannon's on Grand Boulevard. You really ought to stop by there," she retorts. *Who is this woman with Jack? Just when I've worked up the nerve to approach him, it seems too late. Is she competition?* "How do you know Jack?"

"She's a very dear friend of mine," Jack tells her. He twitches his mouth and looks at Alex from the corner of his eyes. *Time to move on, Alex.*

"This is my friend, Mr. Jasper Thomas." Alexandria motions to the man next to her. "Well, enjoy your evening folks. We're late for our reservation."

As time passes, Jack is undaunted by Kelly's behavior. He has faith that it will only get better and better. Indeed, as time passes, she seems to have been transformed by love. Her odd behavior and momentary lapses are seen less and less.

Emma concedes that God has been working. She realizes that she needed to let go and trust. She is also delighted at the change in Kelly and in discussion with Jack at her home, she poses a question to him.

"Well?"

"Well, what?" Jack asks.

"Well, hmmm, let me see. How do I ask this...?" Emma thinks about it. "When did you take her to the promised land?"

All his pearly whites are showing as he shakes his head. "With all due respect, shouldn't you be asking your daughter these private questions and not me?" he asks. "I wouldn't ask my daughter's boyfr--well, maybe I would, being who I am--but Mrs. Sanders', your daughter's a grown woman."

"Yes, and she doesn't have a father. I'm acting as the proxy here. She's grown, but she's different, and I'm trying to see if I can indeed trust you."

"Ma'am, please don't misplace your trust. I'm just a man subject to failure. Trust God," Jack says. "I'm not here to exploit your daughter in her weakness. After all this time, do you think that's my intention?"

She stares him down.

"Okay, okay. Well, we have... not done that. We're still in the un-promised land." He does a half-smile, feeling like a little kid being asked if he took cookies from the cookie jar. "Indeed, being human I've most certainly, unequivocally been tempted. Frankly, I have had plenty of opportunities, and as you can probably attest to, that kind of discipline is not easy for a man nor a woman. But hey, it's not impossible, or he would have said that no man can resist the flesh when he is tempted. Though I've failed in that area many times before, I've prayed intensely for strength to handle this the right way with Kelly."

Emma listens attentively as he continues. "We as men think there's power in our pants and we have to prove something with as many women as we can. We don't understand who we really are, where our real power lies. Once we understand whose image we are created in we can be the leaders we were meant to be. Sex was created for spouses. I've had many soul ties I've had to get broken. Had to get rid of a lot of baggage to prepare for this. Your daughter, well, she's just so innocent. There's something deep within her that I don't want to break. It's not time yet, and I'm trying to be a better man. And besides, I believe you do have a little trust in me, don't you?"

"Well yeah, just a little," Emma confesses. "That's why I asked. I would have known anyway from her. I merely wanted to hear from you." She grins. "A change is very evident in her. She's more mature in her thinking and ways. Even her attitude and dress have changed."

"Well, I've been trying to help your daughter expand in the direction you started as her loving mother. Yes, she is different than when I first laid my eyes on her. But it's not my doing. It's God. And touching back on that private subject, we're going to have plenty of time for that land. That is why I am here, tonight."

Emma stares at Jack, confused.

"Ms. Sanders, please have a seat. As you know Kelly and I are very fond of each other. Quite simply, I love her with all my heart, and I know she feels the same. When I stood before you in our first conversation and I asked you not to hide her away, I knew there was something about her."

Emma grabs a tissue from her pocket for she knew what was coming.

"Yes, there have been some challenging times, to say the least, but she has had to put up with me, also. She has grown so much, and I would like for us to continue on this journey together. I have prayed about this, and so...without further ramblings, Ma'am... May I please have the honor of your daughter's hand in marriage?"

Emma's knees give way to the floor as Jack reaches out to grab her.

"I'm okay, really. I need to sit a bit," she says. "My,

my, I felt this day coming, but it's only been, well, not yet a year, Jack. Is it time?"

"Oh, it's time alright." Jack smiles. "My grace for singleness is over."

"Well okay, oh my, I'm so overwhelmed right now—in a good way. I have one thing to request of you, Jack. As you stand before me this day, promise me something. Promise me that you will not hurt her! If things get rough and she loses her way, will you stand? If you were to look back and wonder why you chose my daughter, will you remember this day and will you stand? This is your time to be the most honest you've ever been in your life, forget the politics, this is real stuff. Can you say *yes* to me?"

A speechless Jack looks at Emma and sees not only the passion but also the fear in her eyes. For a quick second, he begins to indeed wonder what the future could hold. He hears his brother's words, "You can't take on someone like that. What are you trying to prove?"

His mother's voice comes, "Follow your heart."

He then hears the still small voice, *"I am with you."*

He catches his breath as his peace returns. "I will stand!"

They look at each other, and Ms. Sanders starts to cry as they embrace.

"I would have never thought this would happen to my baby girl. Never in a trillion years, though I prayed for it. I am so overwhelmed with joy! My God makes all things beautiful in His time, yes indeed. Have you discussed this with your parents, yet?"

"No, I wanted you to be the first to know and get your blessing," he says. "I'm speaking to them tomorrow. Also, I'm going to formally introduce her to the public and propose to her on election night, whether I win or lose."

"Do you *really* think that's wise, surprising her like that?" Emma asks.

"Oh, I think she can handle it--I really think so." Jack reaches for Emma's hand. "Let her go, Ms. Sanders. She's ready to go, and so am I. She's mine now, my responsibility."

"You indeed have my blessing!" Emma says with a smile. "But that's only one down. There's still two to go."

Jack chuckles. "Can't help you there."

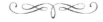

At his parent's home, the following day he breaks the news about the pending engagement to his mom.

"Mom, please take a seat. The time has come, and I really think you know what I'm about to say. You know how I feel about Kelly, and I can surely tell you she feels the same toward me. I have come to understand her, and well, I want to spend my life with her. The only thing to do now is to move forward, hand in hand, to see where this journey will lead." He pauses. *Should I tell her now that we will probably have to adopt children?* "And, well, there's something else I need to tell you." He lowers his head. "We will have kids, but they will be adopted as Kelly is not able to bear children."

The smile leaves his mother's face; she looks squarely into his eyes but then smiles again. "Well, in that case, the more, the merrier. How many am I gonna get? Maybe, I can start a daycare. I've certainly got the space."

"Mom, you always seem to know just the right thing to say, don't you?"

She hugs him. "I'm glad you're not letting that hurdle stop you."

"I plan to ask her hand in marriage during election night."

"Honey, this is your life and your decision to make, and you've already made it. Seems rather quick but had you come to me before deciding, I would have still given you the same words. First, I know you have prayed because marriage is not to be entered into lightly. Second, I know you, and you wouldn't have come to this decision unless you truly believed that this woman was God sent. You've always done what you believed in. We've raised you that way. Obviously, your heart is to do her good and vice-versa."

"Moreover, yes, I had reservations in the very beginning, but I started to see something in you that I'd never seen before, so I let it go. You believe in this relationship, and I believe in you, so that's good enough for me. You know I've grown to love her, as well. I would be proud to have her as my daughter. Please remember, your marriage--though second to God--comes above all and anyone else. Oh, and get marriage counseling, that is a must."

It's as if the air has been released from the balloon. Jack is relieved, and as she hugs him, her eyes tear up.

He hath made everything beautiful in his time.
- Ecclesiastes 3:11

CHAPTER 11

THE CAMPAIGN HAS BEEN moving along at full speed and Election Day is a month away. Jack has to intensify his campaign strategy. He spends the month speaking and listening to his constituents about the continued need for change. Kelly has to take a backseat for a little while, and she's very supportive.

"You're doing great," Jack praises, pressing his lips to Kelly's forehead. "I need you to hang in there with me for just a bit longer, okay?"

"You know I will. I've said it before, and I'll reiterate. I believe in you!"

"Thank you, babe!"

Jack's opponent has painted him as an inexperienced pretty choirboy. Clark Hester's record has placed him as an experienced corruptor, who has never been convicted. It is one day before the election. At a rally with a crowd of supporters, Mr. Hester is speaking. "My opponent, choirboy Jack drinking that baby milk, keeps hinting at the fact that there have been some around me involved in... well, let's just say some things they shouldn't have come close to. They got caught with hands in the cookie jar and their pants, well, not pulled up all the way, and that's putting it nicely. But we won't rehash the details here. How would I know how that money ended up in their personal accounts? Oops, I said no details, didn't I? And you know he's been trying to pin the old guilt-by-association deal on me! Now you all know the legal process took its course and who came out unscathed? What does that tell you? It's been said that some covered for me and are sittin' in jail today because of it. For what reason would they have to lie if I'm not guilty, right?"

The crowd listens attentively.

"I refused to take the lie detector test because of the indignity. It should have never come to that. There's nothing to prove. I've been doing this job for a long time, and I've got a lot left within me. I know the system; I'm comfortable in the role, and I have made progress. Besides, a man is innocent until he's proven guilty. Were those items and money found in *my* possession?"

"Thatta' boy, Hester," says a face in the crowd,

through cheers and applause, his famous campaign slogan.

"Down with baby milk," chants another.

"If you agree with me, then I know I'll have your support, and we will continue to make this district and the state of Mississippi great. We still have more work to do; I am well aware. Thank you for your support."

"We want Clark! We want Clark! We want Clark!" the crowd chants. "Who has our back, Clark does. Who has our back, Clark does."

Across town, Jack is speaking. "People, you said you wanted fresh new blood. You said you wanted introduction of legislation that reflects change for yourselves and future generations. You want low unemployment. You are so tired of fat lard, inflated empty talk, and—you also said if the latter is what I've got then don't bother. Maybe I should go get a job at the local burger joint, right?"

The crowd laughs.

"I know this town, and I know it well. I grew up here as most of you. I've not been in politics all my life as my opponent has. We've all seen jobs and services leave this state, and our tax base erode. Yes, property taxes have increased, but wages have not. This is not fair to you nor our current businesses, and to those that would relocate here ensuring more jobs. Our young people need employment, not tomorrow but right now. Crime has increased tenfold in the last decade."

"Because of our fiscal crises, I've seen—or shall I say, we've seen—schools fail and close in areas where they were sorely needed. Schools that could have been turned around with equal education funding. Oh, did I say that word, haha, yes equal, (he spells the word out) E-Q-U-A-L. Come on, spell it with me E-Q-U-A-L. I have some ideas on how to turn this city and district around, but it's going to take more than just one person to make it work. That's where you all come in. I need you to support your local businesses. I need you to be a part of my voice. Knock on those doors. Talk to your neighbors. Get the word out. There's a new voice that really wants to take your concerns to the state government to finally be heard. I hear you."

Jack sees heads nodding--the people seem to be in agreement with what they're hearing.

"I have met with you on every occasion that would allow. I have listened to your concerns and ideas, and I have taken notes. I have presented my ideas, and I won't forget what you elect me to do. I will fight for this district. I will fight for this state. Please fight with me in this election--and if the title of *baby milk* comes with it, I'll drink it. We don't need shady characters. Show the great state of Mississippi you've had enough. Thank you all and whatever happens tomorrow, never give up trying 'cause I won't."

The crowd roars, "Change has come! Change has come! Hester, Hester you are done."

"Change has come..."

The next day Jack requests that his family, along with Kelly and her family, join him for the election results later that evening. As they're gathered at a local hotel, it seems as if he is winning by a large margin. Still, his heart is in his mouth. The polls finally close. His family and the Sanders' are by his side, waiting. He will not be satisfied until the last vote is in as if a large margin is not enough. Finally, Hester being ashamed at having no chance at overtaking Jack, concedes easily. Jack is declared the winner. He is humbled and overjoyed. Antonio is so proud as Laurie cries and hugs Kelly.

"Thank you, God! Thank you and thank you and you and you and you," he excitedly says as he points to the crowd. The crowd roars. "We did it! You did it! Please work with me. This is for you. I won't always get it right, but it will always be my intention. It will get better, slowly but surely. I can promise that!"

As he finishes his acceptance speech, he reveals that there is one more thing he needs to accomplish. He motions to Kelly and invites her to come to the stage.

"There is someone I would like to formally introduce to you--someone very, very special to me. Some of you may have heard how wonderful she is and yes, it's true. I believe that destiny brought the two of us together. God has put something in each and every one of us that makes us unique. I am an overcomer by his grace and this woman standing beside me, Kelly Denise Sanders, has overcome even more so. Many have witnessed a transformation, and I am more than elated to have been a part of it. So, without further ado..." Jack turns toward the reluctant Kelly and grabs her hands to steady her. "Kelly, I have something to ask of you. You are my world and with that..." Jack takes a deep breath and gets down on one knee. "May I please have the pleasure of being your husband?"

Kelly stares at Jack, speechless.

"Kelly, will you marry me?"

"Jack, I..." she pauses as her moisture filled palms slip out of his hands. There is a blank stare. He was so sure of the smooth-sailing of this scenario as he had played it over and over in his mind.

Gaining poise, he tries again. "Perhaps, I need to rephrase the question." He jokes, and the audience laughs. "Kelly, would you do the honor of being my wife? Please, say yes."

She takes a deep breath then reaches for his hand with tears in her eyes. "Yes," she cries. "Yes, and yes!"

The audience breaks into a thunderous applause. Jack stops holding his breath and slips the ring on her finger. "You can tell this was not rehearsed right!" he jokes.

There is amusement, raucous laughter, and loud applause. Jack and Kelly embrace. Their families are elated. The exciting evening comes to an end as Jack drives his fiancé home.

"I'm so proud and excited for you. You won, baby! You did it! And wow, I can't believe you did that to me." Kelly looks at her ring with a wide grin. "You sure surprised me. I was not expecting that. You won the seat you worked so hard for, and you want to be one with me. Ecstatic is an understatement, right now!"

He wipes her moist face with his hands as he is also overcome with emotion. "Not as ecstatic as I am," he says, grinning.

She wraps her arm around his and lays on his shoulder during the drive home.

"There's one more thing," Jack says, carefully. "I would like for us to visit a doctor. I want to know exactly what's going on. And if there's really no way we can have children, then we'll adopt when the time comes. Is that okay?"

Looking at him, she smiles. "Okay."

CHAPTER 12

LYING IN BED GOING through her mail, Alexandria could not help but notice the rose-colored envelope.

"Hmmm, what do we have here? Looks like an invitation or something. I'll bet my cousin Jackie moved up her wedding date. You leave the country for two months not to be disturbed and look what happens. I told her I wanted to help. But wow, did she really choose rose, really? Oh boy, girl get some class." Her perfectly manicured nails slide under the loose flap easily as she carefully pulls the paper apart. *Yep somebody's getting hitched.* She begins to read, "Kelly Denise Sanders, daughter of Mrs. Emma Sanders and the late Mr. Charles Sanders." Alex pauses as the muscles in her body tighten. "Jaaack Antoniooo Riley, son of Antonio and Laurie Riley request..." She could not bear to finish. "Are you freaking kidding me!"

Grabbing her haircutting scissors from the dresser, she cuts the invite into as many tiny pieces as she can. *His picture from Jackson Politics is coming down tonight from my wall. There was just no time to get my bid in, huh!* She tosses everything into the trash. "Ladies, I'm here to tell ya vision boards don't work. Ugh!"

Jack looks absolutely dashing in grey. The bridesmaids wear rose lace, coordinating with the grey of the groomsmen. Bethel Missionary never looked more beautifully decorated for a special occasion. Beautiful multi-colored roses line the church pews. The presence of a matching rose covered arch is waiting for the special couple. The procession down the aisle starts to the beautiful piano chords of Force Md's "Tender Love" played by a family friend.

As the last bridesmaid and groomsman are midway down the aisle, Kelly does not appear at the sanctuary doors. As her turn nears, a cold sweat permeates throughout her body as she hesitates and runs back to the powder room.

"I, I, I can't do this. I, I, I cannot do this. Wha, wha,

what on earth am I doing? I can't marry him," she cries. "I'm not ready for this. He may be, but I'm not. Wh, wh, why does he want to marry me?"

Kelly runs into an adjacent room and locks the door, crying. Her mother's trying to console her as she tries to force open the door. Uncle Terry's strong arms are no match, either.

"Baby, I'm sorry, but you're acting really silly," Emma speaks through the closed door. "This man wants to be your husband. He has taken the time to get to know you, and he adores what he has found. His eyes and heart passed over many other opportunities, but he stopped when he saw you. Don't run. It's too late. Instead, remind him why he chose you, why he needs you. Don't run, Kelly!"

Emma then reminds her that this is her dream-- what she thought she could never achieve.

"You've come too far, and there's no turning back. You can't come back to my house 'cause I won't let you in, so you better come out of there. Your new life and home awaits. Go get it," Emma says, smiling.

The guest and groom are starting to get a little antsy. The music has stopped. Jack cuts his eyes over at the maid of honor as if to say, "Please, go have a look."

Jessie hurries as Pastor Sims announces, "It's merely a little delay. I'm sure everything will be back on track in only a minute. Thank you for your patience."

Before Jessie gets midway to the back of the church, *Tender Love* starts again. Kelly has reached the back door with her uncle Terry and Emma standing on each side of her. Jack's eyes widen in eager anticipation. His heart is racing. She looks beautiful in a custom made lace couture gown. Her hair is pinned up with small ringlets dangling throughout. She wears her mother's pearl earrings. They've not been touched since Emma married Charles. Kelly stares ahead at Jack and with just a few steps into the aisle she starts to lose composure. Uncle Terry has to hold on tight. She's crying but appears stronger and stronger as she nears her man. This brings tears to her love's eyes.

The pastor says an opening prayer then begins the ceremony. "We are all here today to witness the joining in wedded bliss of Jack Antonio Riley and Kelly Denise Sanders. This truly, truly joyous day celebrates the commitment and love with which Jack and Kelly start their lives together. Through God, you are joined in the holiest of bonds. Marriage is a sacrificial covenant, and it is not to be taken lightly. If any person here can show why these two people should not be joined in holy matrimony, speak now or forever hold your peace." He pauses. "Who gives this woman in holy matrimony to this man?"

Uncle Terry and Emma speak, "We do!"

"Jack, you may begin," says the pastor.

Jack takes a deep breath. "Kelly, the first time I saw you, I knew my search was over. I didn't know what *knowing* you would entail," he laughs and so does the audience. "But God knew I was up to the challenge. He prepared me. So, on this day, I declare my love for you for to know you is to truly love you. You have made me a better man."

Kelly reaches out for a tissue from her mother as Jack wipes her tears. Emma's eyes begin to well up as Antonio embraces his wife. Standing at the altar, Tiffy and Jessie fight back the flow but are overcome, as well.

Pastor Sims pauses momentarily for composure before continuing. "Repeat after me Jack, if you can."

Jack braces himself, sucking back the tears welling up in his eyes. "I, Jack Antonio Riley, take you Kelly Denise Sanders, to be my lawful wedded wife, to have and to hold from this day forward, for better, for worse, for richer, for poorer, in sickness and in health, until death do us part. I pledge to be true to you in good times and in bad."

"Kelly, you may begin," says the pastor.

With shaking hands, she manages to get out her words slowly.

"Take your time," the pastor encourages.

"J-J-J-J-Jack, you are truly....a dream come true. Uh, most days I have to pinch myself for this miracle. How, how could I, me, be soooo blessed. Your love and patience are unmatched because I know what I've put you through. What may yet come our way, I-I don't know, but I thank God for you wanting to take this journey with me. I will try very hard not to make you regret it."

"Kelly, please repeat after me," says the pastor. "I, Kelly Denise Sanders, take you, Jack Antonio Riley, to be my lawful wedded husband, to have and to hold from this day forward, for better, for worse, for richer, for poorer, in sickness and in health, until death do us part. I pledge to be true to you in good times and in bad."

The rings are exchanged.

"What God has put together, let no man put asunder," the pastor concludes. "By the power vested in me by God and the state of Mississippi, I now pronounce you man and wife. You may finally salute your beautiful bride."

"Please don't bite me," he teases.

She laughs. "Not a chance."

Jack embraces his bride as tightly as he could as Kelly twists and turns to get wiggle room. The guests are amused. Their passionate kiss seems to last into eternity until the pastor taps Jack on his shoulder.

"That's enough, you've proved your point. We get it."

Their audience laughs then let out a roaring cheer.

The pictures have been taken and dinner has been served. After eating just a salad and dessert, Jack takes to the dance floor by himself. He requests a special song. The smooth and soothing intro of *Sensitivity* by Ralph Tresvant begins as he removes his jacket, tossing it on the floor. Taking his time, he loosens his tie and unbuttons the top buttons of his shirt before rolling up his sleeves.

What in the world is my husband about to do?

He starts swaying to the rhythmic and melodic beat. Kelly covers her eyes, then her mouth in disbelief. She bobs her head to the music, swaying back and forth. The ladies gather around her in awe as they clap to the beat, mesmerized.

"Is that your man, Kelly?" Jessie cheers. "What happened to his two left feet?"

His sleek black lace up's slide across the floor in fluid motion then slide back into the moonwalk. He's never seen Kelly laugh so hard. He reaches for her hand and whispers in her ear, "Sens..i..tiv..i..ty." He then draws back to continue his solo act of swirls and fancy footsteps while flailing his arms. Toward the end of the song, he motions for Emma to join him in steppin'.

Shaking her head, she says, "Oh no," *Mama's too old for that.* The ladies push her onto the floor, anyway. Jack grabs her hand, persuading her to join him.

"Didn't know you had it in you, Momma Sanders."

Aww, he called me Momma. She laughs and laughs.

"Me either, son. Oh my goodness, this is so embarrassing. What the pastor must be thinking!"

She called me "son." Jack smiles.

Antonio and Laurie are grinning from ear to ear. Jack knows better than to ask his own mother out to the floor. The prim and proper lady would never oblige to such moves. Carter grabs a lady friend as Jessie and Tiffy join the floor. All the guests follow suit to finish out the song.

Jack reaches for his bride once more, and while pulling her close, he whispers in her ear.

"Hey, Mrs. Riley. Now that you're mine, there's one more thing that would make this night even more special. How about you guess what that is?" He smiles, suggestively. "Why don't we give our thank you's, say our goodbyes, and blow this reception? I am sooo ready, baby girl!"

Kelly flashes a half-smile, causing the big grin on his face to retreat.

The Fairvine Inn outside the city awaits their arrival. Though she has prayed about this night, she stiffens in anticipation. While the new bride's body is there, her mind has yet to check in as Jack starts to embrace her.

"I love you, Kelly."

Wrestling her jittery body out of his reach, she heads into the bathroom. The click of the door lock is heard behind her retreat.

"Oh, I see, you're trying to get ready for this historic special occasion, your grand entrance, I get it."

Time passes, and Kelly still hasn't come out of the bathroom.

"Whatcha doing in there lady?"

She has been sitting on the side of the tub, stalling. "Uh...I'm going to take a shower."

"Can you please come out? Please...pretty please." Lowering his voice to almost a whisper, "Pretty, pretty, pretty please with sugar on top?"

Twenty more minutes pass, and he is worn out from asking and finds himself nodding off. Kelly has fallen asleep on the floor in the bathroom. When Jack awakens, he finds that she is not next to him in bed. Banging on the bathroom door, he calls out to her. "Kelly, are you alright?"

There is no response; he can't get the door open, and kicking proves fruitless. He hurriedly calls security. Jack finds his bride lying on the floor, motionless. Touching her, she has no choice but to respond. Her game was up, as he realizes he's been bamboozled. She hadn't wanted to lose her senses, but fear crept in at the most inconvenient moment for Jack and for her. After confirming she's all right, security leaves. Grinning as they leave, they've made up their versions of what just took place and cannot hold back the smiles.

Jack leads his new wife to bed as she's crying hysterically. Silly is an understatement as to her feelings at the moment for what she just put her husband through. Wrapping his arms around her, he consoles his bride as they both fall asleep. As morning arises, there is frustration on both sides.

"I won't hurt you. I promise," Jack says, raising her hand and pointing to her wedding ring. He then points to his band before placing a hand over his own heart. In a gentle voice, he reminds her of their vows. Her eyes are glued to him. She understands exactly what he means.

"I love you, Jack." Reaching out to hold his hand, she finally relents. Jack is more than relieved and to her surprise, so is his bride.

Whoa, I felt like I was taking candy from a baby!

The hunt has started for a new home. The couple is anxious to move out of Jack's-toy box- condo, as he liked to call it. Kelly is given the task of finding listings in their price range, in conjunction with their agent. After one exhausting unsuccessful day of house hunting, she starts the search again for the perfect home. She hands Jack the list and as he looks it over, he finds they are the exact same homes that they've already explored.

"Kelly, you're joking, right?" he asks, playfully.

She looks at the list. "I did my research again and found these. What's the problem?"

"Honey, look at the list one more time. Does anything look familiar to you?" He hands her the paper, and she examines it.

"Why no, should it?"

"I'll tell you what, we will get together with the agent and generate an even bigger list," he says, lovingly. "Thanks for all your hard work, honey."

Ignoring the knot in his stomach, he brushes the incident off as an every now and then occurrence which is bound to happen. He happily determines not to think too much of it.

After settling on a red brick Georgian, not far from his parent's home, the couple is relieved to move in. More closet space is a Godsend to Kelly to cater to her husband's wardrobe. She often teases him about his habit. Unpacking boxes one evening, a sudden urge takes over her body and is relentless. Stopping to peer at her husband, she lovingly raises his hand and points to his wedding band. He takes note of hers as she extends her hand, then points to her chest. She nods in agreement. He's beside himself with amusement. Excited about his newfound teaching skills, she leads him to the bedroom.

"I taught you well, didn't I? My my, now we're talkin'."

God Has Spoken – Hebrews 1: 1-2

CHAPTER 13

WITH PASSING MONTHS, the new Mrs. Riley finds herself adjusting to married life well. They are extremely happy as prayer, special attention and patience have caused her to thrive. Jack asks her to quit her secular work temporarily so as not to overwhelm her. She's enjoying the newfound freedom of her own home while reveling in homemaking decisions. Unveiling a talent for decorating, she furnishes their home beautifully. Her mother-in-law's home is a source of inspiration, to Jack's amusement.

"Jack, am I losing it? I found a beautiful paisley chair at Digby's for your study. I placed it in there this morning, but now it's gone. I can't find it in the house, anywhere. Why did you move it and where?"

Jack pulls her close and offers a gentle smile. "I think it's really sweet that you admire my mother's taste, but I would really like to see something other than browns and tans in *our* home."

Kelly feels a bit disappointed considering neutral colors were safe, and it didn't take as much creativity. "Why is that?" she asks.

"I guess, those colors remind me of my childhood home," Jack explains. "This home is *our* safe haven with our rules and our tastes. You don't have to emulate anyone. You can choose any color *except* tan and brown. I won't mind. I trust your creativity."

"You got rid of the chair?"

"I put it in the garage," he confesses, squirming. "I hate paisley."

"Fair enough." Kelly wraps her arms around Jack's neck. "How do all red walls sound?"

Jack tickles Kelly, and she bursts into laughter.

Pastor Sims asks if Kelly can work with the young children as a volunteer at church. She happily accepts the call on a part-time basis. Emma is overcome with joy at the continual change in her daughter.

"Look at what God has done!" Emma cheers. "If

only her father could only see her now."

As the years pass, working with her little mini buddies, as she likes to call them, Kelly begins to feel something is still missing--nagging at her soul. The longing for a child is growing stronger with each passing day. Every doctor's appointment assures the couple that her body cannot support a child. Her uterus is badly deformed, and yet dreams of pregnancy seem to be taking over her mind, anyway. Feeling downcast, her concerns are brought before the Lord for the millionth time.

"Father God, I know that you hear me as I so humbly come to you with this need. I cannot bear to leave this spot until I hear from you, one way or another." Tearing up, she continues. "You know my longing for a child and my condition and what the doctors have said." Before she could finish speaking, she feels the answer deep within her.

Daughter, I've put that desire in you. It is me responding to your wants. Now is the time to receive it by faith. I'm saying "Yes" but what are you saying?

Covering her mouth in surprise, she thanks the Lord and wonders how to approach her husband. Her excitement won't let her wait. Kelly rushes into his office.

He looks so studious and involved as he's reading. Maybe this is not the right time, but I can't keep this to myself.

Mounds of paperwork hide his new desk though

he tries so hard to keep it tidy. Beams from the sun are pouring in on his back, but he doesn't seem to mind. It bothers her, so she closes the blinds halfway.

Jack looks up. "Thank you, my back was feeling a little warm, but I was too lazy to get up."

"I need to talk to you about something." She didn't give him a chance to tell her he was busy at the moment. "I've been feeling a certain kind of way, recently."

"Well, okay." He sits back, crossing his arms. Kelly pulls up a chair and sits in front of him. "I'm all ears," he says.

"I-I-I-I'm ready for a child. I-I-I want to carry a child!"

Jack pushes himself back, annoyed. "What did you say?"

"I want to carry a child."

"Why are you even bringing this up? We both sat in the doctor's office as he explained our situation. I saw with my own eyes what they've been telling you. Baby, I am sorry, but nothing has changed. It's okay, though. We're going to adopt when the time is right."

"Jack, people have told me that my life would always be different than everyone else's, but look at my life now!" She reaches for his hand. "I'm sure you never thought you would be attracted to and married to someone like me."

Jack's face takes on a contorted look with flared nostrils. "Don't you ever, ever, say something like that again." He grabs her face and pulls her close. "There is nothing wrong with you. I don't believe I have ever put you down or made you feel like you didn't measure up. I'm sorry, but don't ever say that again. All I ever wanted was to be your safest place in the world, next to God. I love you. You are a gift to me."

She smiles. "You are a gift to me as well." She rubs her eyes. "But I'm sorry, I can't let this go. I hear you, Jack, I do. And I have been hearing the doctor's all my life, but I feel as if something has changed. In fact, I know it has! I've been to the throne in prayer, and I really wish you would do the same in agreement with me."

He stares at her for a moment, compassion taking over. "Baby, your concerns are of the utmost importance to me--"

"Then, take my side in this."

He sighs. "Tell you what... I'm going to pray more earnestly about this, and when we revisit this conversation, I'll tell you how I feel about it, okay?" He stands with a stack of papers in his hand, but as he turns, he trips over a cord that was on the floor. Kelly didn't mean to smirk, but she couldn't help it. "Are you alright, honey?"

He picks himself up, brushes his hands over his pants and leaves the room.

My husband's two left feet are back in action, I see.

Kelly tries to give her husband space, but as the month progresses the tension-filled atmosphere becomes almost unbearable. Kelly is noticeably quieter and somber, and Jack just doesn't know how to make her feel better. Having had enough, he is compelled to pray as he said he would.

"Well, Lord, we are doing so wonderful at this time. I really don't want her to start flipping out about having a child, so what do I do?" Jack begs. "Can you make this possible? You've done it for others. Can it really happen for us? Why is it so hard sometimes to believe for others but not for ourselves?"

Kelly's inspired to begin decorating the spare bedroom. Jack arrives home one evening and asks, "What on earth are you doing?"

"I'm preparing our baby's room in faith," she says. "I think the crib would fit nicely in that corner and my favorite rocking chair would go right next to it, right here. What do you think?"

Jack lowers his head and walks away. Knowing it was not his best response, he reasons that it would be better to leave than to speak his mind and hurt her feelings.

She is undeterred and tells him so. She tries to entice him later that evening. "Come on Jack, let's go make a baby."

He wants to lash out, *You are not going to have a*

child of your own, so quit it now, but he knows that would be insensitive. He doesn't want to hurt her feelings.

"Honey, do you want to go baby gear shopping tomorrow?" she presses.

"Kel, I'm sorry but can we talk about this some other time, please? I'm in the middle of something, right now."

Jack fears this may eventually become a setback for her progress. Understanding something has to change, and quickly, he continues to pray for more guidance as he speaks with his family as well as hers. He asks their thoughts on adoption as he knew there was no other way, at least in his mind. He pours forth all his fears. "Can she really handle a child? Is she indeed stable enough at this point? Is it the right time?" Both families tell him that all these questions can best be answered by God.

He sits Kelly down and brings up the subject of adoption, again.

"Adoption? Why do you keep talking about adoption? I want to have my own child. I mean, *our* own. God said *yes,* Jack! I'm telling you, he said *yes.* Please, believe with me."

"What's wrong with adopting?" he asks.

"Nothing! I know there are beautiful children out there waiting for a loving family. Adoption is a beautiful thing, and I would not mind for our second child, but let's give it some time okay, let's believe?"

He closes his eyes, briefly. "Kelly, I prayed about this, I swear. But I'm still fearful."

"You've got to believe with your whole heart like I do. How can two walk together unless they agree? What happened to your faith?"

"I do have faith. I know it's possible, but..."

"No buts Jack. It will happen for us. I'm telling you, we're having a baby and it will be a boy. How does Jack Grayson Riley Jr. grab you?"

Jack smiles. "So, you want a mini-me? Isn't one Jack enough?" he teases, grinning from ear to ear.

"There ought to be many more like you in this world." She wiggles into his arms. "I'm a very blessed woman, indeed. Have I told you that lately? Not many men could be so selfless, sacrificial, patient and understanding. Not many, my love."

He rubs his finger under her eye to catch a tear. "It means the world to me that you think that."

"If our son grows up to be half the man you are, it would still be enough."

Jack smiles, brightly. "You're perfect for me, and to me. I really need you to believe that. I've learned a lot from you, babe. I'm the blessed one in this room. I can be patient but you know I can also be pretty darn impetuous at times, too."

"I just had a thought," she says. "You ought to write a book, Jack. God has graced you with so much wisdom and compassion."

"Hmm, only if I can keep your sister, Tiffy, out of it.

Besides yourself, your mother makes for a very interesting character though."

Kelly laughs. "That's not nice about my sister." She reaches out to grab his firm and reassuring hands. "Honey, touch my belly and tell me that the fruit of my womb is blessed."

He rubs his hands over her perfectly flat and toned stomach knowing there is no turning back now. "The fruit of your womb is mightily blessed, my love," he says, smiling.

She lays her head on his chest and melts into his warmth. "How about we put our faith into action?"

He smiles, seductively. "Are you saying you want to make a baby, right now?"

"No, silly." She pulls back and laughs. "I want to go shopping and turn the spare bedroom into a nursery."

Jack laughs. "Of course, that was my next thought."

Jack Jr.'s room is finished beautifully with red cherry furnishings. Neutral mint green and white are chosen for the walls. Kelly asks that the germy carpet be removed and replaced with ceramic tile. A tree mural with rainbow leaves is on one wall. The inscription of family member's names will grace each leaf. Little white bunnies and sheep cover the green wall behind the crib. The name of Jack Grayson Riley graces the wall above the décor. A large stuffed beagle hides in the corner, next to a rocking chair. Another wall holds the dresser with pictures of angels on each side. The joy in Jack's heart is tremendous in these moments. Indeed, as he decorated the room, his faith has increased tremendously. This was his gentle push of faith in action that God had planned, all along. His faith to believe as he had prayed for.

Family members ask to see the finished results, but Jack has one request for each of them. "If you're not in agreement with us then please, don't enter our son's room. No negative vibes here."

In the following days, Jack is busy with legislative tie-ups. Kelly enthusiastically pledges to check once at the beginning of each month for evidence of her little boy. She never doubts in her faith upon the negative results of five months of testing. But upon the beginning of the sixth month, she goes through the familiar ritual of a check and a repeat check. The last check yields something she has not seen before. She is in shock so she repeats the test a second time, then a third time to believe what she sees.

Jack is in bed supposedly reading but half asleep. A sudden nerve-rattling scream jars him with extreme alarm. Bounding out of bed, he trips over his blanket. His hand slips off the dresser as he hits the floor landing on his knees. She's at the top of the stairs by the time he gets up. Stunned, he looks at her, and she seems to be alright.

"What's wrong? Why did you scream like that?"

She jumps into bed with a happy glee, and he sits next to her. "Are you alright old man?"

"I'm okay," as he rubs his chest, "Just a bruised ego I suppose."

"We are having a baby, we are having a baby, we are pregnant!" she shouts, happily.

His jaw drops. "Are you sure?" he asks with excitement rising inside of him.

"I did the test numerous times. I'm sure of it!"

They both start screaming at the top of their lungs, "Ah, ah, ah! God is so good! Thank you, God!"

"Honey, let's confirm our miracle by going to the doctor tomorrow," Jack suggests. "And let's keep this to ourselves until after our appointment. We will tell everyone how far along you are and all the particulars then, okay?"

She promises as much as her heart bursting with excitement would allow.

As they sit in the doctor's office, the doctor is in disbelief. He stares at his patient, imagining who indeed was sitting before him. *She will make a believer out of me*, he thought.

"Mrs. Riley, you are indeed with a child, about three weeks along. I have read the reports of my colleagues on your case but what I'm seeing is totally different from what I've read. The reports state that your uterus is so severely damaged they wanted to remove it, and there were other complications whereby you could not get pregnant nor sustain a pregnancy. I understand this abnormality was present from birth, but we will have to keep a close eye on you. I want to have a closer look at your uterus. We've got to run some tests to see exactly what is going on and make sure you can sustain this pregnancy."

"We'll do whatever you say, doctor," Jack says.

The doctor rubs his hand across his forehead. "This is a bonafide miracle. I can't see any other way to explain it.

"I need to go over your records once again. Will you excuse me?" He gets up.

Jack and Kelly stare at each other. Their grins stretch almost to their ears. "Yes, it is a miracle," Jack whispers more to Kelly than to the doctor.

"Yes, I have to go over your records one more time. I'm repeating myself I know," the doctor says, "Just to be sure, you understand right?"

"My organs are fine, doctor," Kelly spurts out. "I'm going to have my baby."

"Right." The doctor suddenly realizes there will be no reasoning with Kelly. "Well, let's take this one day at a time. We're all on the same page, here."

"We just want our baby to be safe," Jack says.

"Exactly," Kelly agrees.

"Then, you'll need to come for every appointment," the doctors says. "In the meantime, congratulations."

The happy couple leave the office giving praises to God. *"Thank you, my father, God, and Kelly, for not giving up on me when I did not believe,"* exhorts Jack, grinning from ear to ear. *"I know it takes me a while sometimes, yes, it takes me a while. I'm still growing."*

If ye have faith as a grain of mustard seed, ye shall say unto this mountain, Remove hence to yonder place, and it shall remove, and nothing shall be impossible unto you. - Matthew 17:30

Husbands, love your wives, even as Christ also loved the church, and gave himself for it; That he might sanctify and cleanse it with the washing of water by the word, That he might present it to himself a glorious church, not having spot, or wrinkle, or any such thing; but that it should be holy and without blemish.
– Ephesians 5:25-27

CHAPTER 14

LIFE IS GOOD at the Riley household as they prepare for their gift from God. Family members are in awe of the miracle child, and some are moved to seek a closer walk with God. They have seen the changes in Kelly, and now the pregnancy. They cannot deny a higher power is involved.

Emma has fainting episodes with all that is taking place in her daughter's life. *"Lord, this is surely more than I prayed for. She's married, and now she's having a child, my grandchild. They said it was impossible. It has almost been too overwhelming. You are indeed a prayer answering father. You've come through so many times before, how could we not believe?"*

Tiffy and Jessie are delighted as they plan a baby

shower. Looking over the plans, Jessie stops and looks up at Tiffy. "Girl, I thought for sure we would be planning this for *you*."

"Well, I guess I have more sense than you all thought, huh?"

"I have to say Tiff, I love you."

"Wow, I love you too, snob!"

They both crack up.

Kelly is rejoicing in her growing belly. She and Jack find pleasure in measuring it every couple of weeks as the new life grows. Life could not be any better for the couple!

Month seven has arrived, and Jack is away preparing to make a televised speech on behalf of a colleague. Emma, her two daughters, and Laurie have joined Kelly for the viewing at her home. The atmosphere is light and jovial as they all talk about the baby shower. The ladies reduce their chatter as the speech starts. About ten minutes into Jack's speech, Kelly looks down at her swollen belly to massage it. Fear wells up in her as tears start streaming.

"I, I don't think I can handle this. I don't want this baby. I can't handle a child. Why would he let me get pregnant? Jack doesn't want it, either. I can tell, can't you?" A sudden sadness permeates her face as all eyes veer in her direction. Emma's heart skips a beat. An uneasy feeling has entered Kelly's home. All excitement has been released from the atmosphere with one sudden gush. Breaking the stillness, Emma manages to muster a smile from somewhere deep within her. Moving toward her daughter to hug her, Kelly pushes her away.

"Kelly, dear. This is what you prayed for. You're letting fear get the best of you, right now."

"I'm going to give this baby up for adoption."

"Jack won't let you do that," Emma says, firmly. "And neither will we."

"Well, try and stop me, whose body is it?" she challenges.

"You're clearly not feeling well. Why don't we put you to bed." Emma reaches for Kelly, but she pulls away.

"All my confidence is waning. I feel so uneasy. Will I be a good mother?" Kelly asks.

Jack's speech no longer holds their attention.

Kelly's eyes stay focused intensely on her husband as if for quite another reason. "Look at him," she says. "He deserves better."

"Dear, how about we see you off to bed so you can get some rest," Emma tries again. "I think you're emotionally exhausted. The baby may be weighing on you; everything is going to be alright, sweetie. I promise."

"No, I want to finish listening to his speech."

After the viewing, Kelly quickly turns off the set and shouts, "Great words from a great man, right? Wow, why does everyone look so sad? Let's eat. I'm hungry!"

Emma grabs Tiffy's arm before Tiffy has a chance to open her mouth.

"I'll talk to her later, Tiff. Yes, let's feed the baby and ourselves in the process, shall we ladies?" Emma forces a smile as she heads to the table.

The evening proceeds around the kitchen table as hors d'oeuvres are served. There is light conversation along with strained chuckles.

As they prepare to leave, Emma volunteers, "Kelly, dear. I know Jack is not due back until tomorrow, so I'm insisting that one of your sisters stay the night with you. You're seven months now; eight is not far behind. The baby could come this early, you never know. Your husband shouldn't leave you alone so much during these last months. Why look how big you are. Looks like I could be a grandmother any day now!"

Emma's pulse rises, knowing she sounds silly. The other ladies glance at her then lower their heads.

"There's no reason for anyone to stay the night, I'm perfectly fine. Our baby will be born in the right month and on the right day! Mother, you've been acting so strange tonight, are you alright?"

Emma's piercing eyes can be sensed a mile away. She knows Kelly is not in her right mind at present, so she refrains from responding to her comment. Her eyes have done their job. The ladies are more than anxious to leave as Kelly heads off to bed.

Emma prays for peace that evening. *"Lord, my daughter is in such a good place. I pray this continues, especially now with the baby coming."*

The girls decide not to tell Jack of the dismal words his wife spoke that evening. How could they?

"It's just some crazy talk," says Tiffy.

"I'm sure it was just one of those off the wall moments she's prone to. Though, one hasn't reared its ugly head in quite some time," Emma surmises. "It's probably hormonal. Some women are badly affected. It's like they're another person."

"But she seemed so serious," says Jessie, concerned.

"Jessie, I said it's just hormonal. Did you hear me? Just a mindless thought at the moment. Let's keep her confidence up. I don't want to hear no more 'bout it, just pray for her. It's got to be hormonal. It just has to be."

The following weeks things are back to normal. Emma has not heard of any unsettling or awkward outbursts from Kelly, and Jack has not mentioned anything unusual. Perhaps there were things he was keeping to himself. She was too afraid to ask.

Kelly approaches her husband at his desk one evening. "Honey, take a look at this beautiful dress. Isn't it absolutely gorgeous?" She hands him a clipping she tore from a magazine. "Look at the beautiful sensuous silk fabric. I love the champagne color and burgundy roses on the bodice."

Nodding his head in approval, he says, "That's pretty sexy. Are you going to get that for me, only for your man's eyes?"

"Yes, after the baby arrives for our first time together."

"Can't wait for that. Let me have that clipping. I'll keep it in my file for safekeeping."

"Jack, I'd like to talk to you about something."

"I'm all ears."

"Well, to be honest, I, uh... this is hard, very hard. I have been having these unusual feelings about our child. I, I, I re-really don't think I'm ready to be a mother. I don't think I can handle this. I'm scared."

He turns his head away and closes his eyes for a second, but quickly regains composure. "Of course, you're ready. This is what we prayed for, remember? My faith has been strengthened through this. Meeting you and marrying you turned my heart back to God for good. Watching you grow and become the woman you are has changed a lot of lives, especially mine. Now, we're going to be parents! It's a miracle!"

"Jack, something doesn't feel right," she says.

"Something just doesn't feel right."

The muscles in his jaws are stiffening as he tries to utter words. Not willing to guess what would come out of her mouth next and even more unwilling to hear anything else she has to say, he quickly grasps at changing the vibe in the room.

"Honey, you'll be fine, you have what it takes. Now, where's your faith? You've got to be in agreement with me, now. Unless two walk together, how can they agree--sound familiar? Look at me now, look at me. Take my hand. You can do this. You're going to be the best mother there is." He places his hand across her overgrown belly.

"Now, repeat after me. *The mother of this child is blessed with confidence, wisdom, and peace.* Your son is counting on you. He needs you. Go upstairs and get some rest. I'll be up as soon as I can." He glances at his watch. "I've got one hour to finish this report. Oh, and guess who wants to come to dinner tomorrow evening?"

"Who?"

"Carter with the kids and a new lady he would like us to meet. I guess his ex-doesn't mind the kids hanging out with this lady. I believe he said her name is Lilly and that she may be the one, again." He cracks a half smile. "Think you can whip up a fancy feast on such short notice?"

"I absolutely can." She smiles. "And I'm sorry about all the rambling, honey. I'm sure it's hormonal. I've just been feeling a little out of sorts, lately. I'll see what the doctor says at my next appointment."

His body is turned away from her as she leaves the room. Cupping his face, there are a million unsettling thoughts racing through his mind. *"God, I'm praying that this is indeed hormonal. I'm sure she's just a little wired and tired, trying to get through this. The baby is going to change her for the better."*

In the morning, Kelly calls her mom to take her to get groceries for the evening dinner. "I have to whip up a special meal for guests tonight," she tells her mother.

Emma wonders why she is asking for a ride. Jack has hired a special driver to take her wherever she needs to go.

"Are you alright, dear? Feeling okay?" Emma asks nervously.

"Mom, I'm fine. I only need the company of family, is all."

Emma doesn't want to read too much into this. She asks Tiffy to accompany her, instead. Kelly pulls out her grocery list browsing the aisles at *Right Way Mart*. Tiffy watches closely as her sister retrieves way too many items for a meal for four adults and two kids. Near the end of the shopping trip, the cart is filled with eight pounds of ground beef, ten bottles of salad dressing, six large boxes of macaroni, six boxes of cake mix and four dozen eggs.

"Mrs. Kelly Denise Riley, please stop it. Do not pick up another item. Can you read your grocery list out loud to me?" Tiffy asks.

Gazing at Tiffy confused, Kelly asks, "Why do you want me to read it out loud? Here, you take it and read it yourself."

"No, just read what you have, and I'll check it against the cart to make sure you haven't forgotten anything."

"Eight pounds of ground beef, ten bottles of salad dressing, six large boxes of macaroni, six boxes of cake mix, four dozen eggs, 3 gal..."

"Stop," Tiffy tells her.

Feeling faint from holding her breath as not to scream, she releases a long sigh. Tiffy only needs the easy fix of slow breaths to stay stable. Her heart flutters. She did not say a word; she figured there's no use.

As they return home, Kelly mentions, "It's no secret I can put out a great scratch cake with the best of them, but to be quicker I chose cake mix this time. I think I'll start with dessert first."

Tiffy glares at her disturbed sister as Kelly smiles reticently. "Are you feeling okay, Tiffy?" Kelly asks.

"Hmm, ugh, okay, you start with your cake and I'll help with the rest of dinner," Tiffy says.

Kelly cracks a dozen eggs into a bowl, followed by a whole five-pound bag of sugar, followed by eight sticks of butter. As she looks for the hand mixer, Tiffy leaves the room momentarily. Her emotions can no longer be held in check. The seat cushion over her face cannot muffle the sound of crying as she senses her sister may be losing the mental battle she fought so hard to win. Only this time the vengeance is the worse she's ever witnessed. Half drying her tears, she returns to the kitchen. She grabs Kelly's hands and pulls them away from the mixer.

"Kelly, stop. Let's forget about dessert, right now. Let's just concentrate on dinner. Please, let me help with the meatloaf. Now, of course, that's my specialty," says Tiffy with a smile.

"Okay, well, you work on the meatloaf. I want to continue with Jack's cake," Kelly insists.

Tiffy's hands fly up in a wring your neck motion. She turns her back to her sister, momentarily. Kelly senses something is wrong, but she doesn't understand the concern. She finally admits she is feeling a little run down.

"I think I'm going to lie down for a few minutes," Kelly says.

"Yes, please do that! I mean, this is such a large undertaking. It's okay to leave it to me. Go get some rest, sweetie." Feeling as if she may pass out again, Tiffy drops into the nearest chair. "God, we need you!"

Jack calls to check in on the dinner plans. Tiffy is

purposely slow about answering the phone. She's fine with letting the sound echo until it stops. *Oh my, I forgot, don't want it to bother Kelly. Better answer it.*

"Hey Tiff, it's me, your favorite politician, didn't know you were there!"

Tiffy breathes another sigh.

"What's the sigh all about?"

"Oh, it's nothing."

"Tiffy, you are not being forthcoming. You were never a good liar. What's up, lady?"

"Ugh, I think you need to cancel dinner plans for tonight."

"Why, is Kelly alright? What's going on, what is it?"

"Brother, she's resting now, but I would not say that alright is the best word to use. I would not say that, at all. She's okay for now. She's resting."

Tiffy pushes the recliner chair all the way back as she pauses. She really didn't want to repeat what she had witnessed. It would hurt to retell it, but she had no choice as she looks around for tissues.

"Ohhh, okay. I see…" Squinting his eyes shut as he's playing the scenes in his mind. "Can you please stay with her a little while longer? Umm, I'll be there… well, as soon as I can." Exasperated, he quickly hangs up.

Looking up, he senses a dark, ominous cloud rising up to overtake him. *This is very disturbing, rather extreme behavior. Keep it together, Jack.*

He calls Carter to cancel the plans for the night

without giving him major details.

"Kell's not feeling well," is all he can manage to muster.

"No worries," says Carter. "We'll meet up soon."

CHAPTER 15

JACK'S SPIRIT IS HEAVY. He does not want to entertain a sour spirit in his home upon his return but he understands life at the Riley's may be changing. This does not sit well. His wife's behavior has never been as acute. *It has to be the pregnancy. Once it's over, she'll be okay,* he assures himself. *I will get her under medical care.*

He stops at Bannigan's Bar a few blocks from home for a quick drink; feeling a diversion is called for. Though this one was certainly not in his best interest, he knew. The first inclination of a call to his pastor or a trusted friend passes quickly. The bartender starts chatting up a heavy conversation on politics, but Jack isn't in the mood for political strategy. The place is nearly empty, but he wishes his new found friend would talk to some other patron. The one time he wishes he could fade into the background, he can't. Finishing his drink, he thanks the bartender and leaves a tip.

"Hi, Congressman Riley. Didn't think I'd ever see you here." A customer recognizes Jack as he's about to leave and walks over to greet him.

"Hi, how are ya?" Jack responds.

"I'm doing great, just wanted to say glad you're working for us. I was at your town hall meeting the other day, and yeah, you're right, progress has been slow but at least there has been progress. I can attest to that. The projects that are going on are well noted, and you said there's more to come with extra money that's been earmarked for the state. The property tax bill is finally on the agenda, as well. Whoo hoo! I'm proud of myself. I keep up with that kind of stuff, you know. Just want to say thank you for these years that have been well spent."

"Well, thanks for your kind words but I don't work alone. I really have to get going now. Thanks, again." As he's headed toward the door, Alexandria Mitchell happens to walk in and spots him immediately. Laser focused and deep in thought, he's about to walk past her.

Oh my, my lucky day! And it appears he's alone, too. She extends the palm of her hand toward his face in a stopping motion. "Hi, Jack. Fancy meeting you here.

Are you leaving, already, are you alone, why are you here?" she asks.

"Hi, Alex. I'm minding my business. Yeah, fancy meeting you too, but I'm about to leave."

"Wait, don't go. Have a drink with me. I'm buying." She smiles. "Come on, just one, what's the harm in that, business partner?"

"Well... okay, just one more won't hurt, I guess."

They take a seat at a nearby table. "So, good-looking, what brings you here? I'm a regular and this is the first time I've seen you. I didn't think you were the bar type, being happily married and all." She laughs.

The corners of his mouth barely move.

"Are you okay? You don't seem your usual cheerful self?" she notices.

"I'm okay, I kind of have a situation I'm trying to come to grips with. Need to figure out the best way to handle it."

"Wow, anything you care to share, is it business?" she asks.

"No, it's not."

"Well, I know we don't get a chance to talk often, and I haven't lived a lot of years, but in those years I've done a lot of living. I believe I've gained some wisdom. Tell you what, why don't you stop by my place and you can tell me all about your situation. This doesn't seem like the best place to share your concern. You seem so down. You need a pep talk. Let me help."

He looks at her and pauses momentarily. *Maybe people have been reading her wrong all these years. Maybe she does have some compassion and understanding. Maybe, there's a heart in that little frame. After all, she is human--subject to change.*

But she hasn't changed Jack, has she? Run Jack, Run.

He ignores that check in his spirit as the muscles in his neck start to tighten.

Jack, stop being a coward. Face your fears and go home to your wife.

But we're just going to talk, no harm in that, is there?

Don't be naïve, man.

"Ugh, sure we can talk, but I'd rather not go to your place."

"Well, I'm parked on the corner at Broad Street," she tells him. "You could just walk me to my car?"

"Okay. That I can do."

"Nice ride you got here, it's the M5, right? The government pays you pretty well for your political passion, don't they?"

"Why don't you sit in it and check it out?" she offers.

As he gets into her car, his legs feel as if 50 lb weights are suddenly stacked on top of them. "This is nice. You've got every feature imaginable in here."

"Yeah, you were talking about passions. Politics is one, but it's certainly not my only passion, Jack. I have many, many others," she says as she looks into his eyes. "I live only 10 minutes away. Are you sure you don't want to stop by?"

"I'm very sure."

"Geez, I don't bite."

"So, what I wanted to talk to you about. Okay, so here's the situation. Someone I know is having a really hard time with..." *Click.* Jack hears the sound of the car doors locking.

"Why did you lock the doors?" Jack pulled on the handle. "Open 'em right now."

"The master lock is on my side, dear, just like the windows. You would have to crawl over me to get to them."

She slides over and pushes in a little too close to Jack as his heart starts to race. The car seems to be getting smaller, but it was her moving in fast without mercy and relentless. He's trying to hold her back with one arm while using his other hand to fumble with the door handle.

"What's wrong with you, you need help, seriously, stop it, stop it. Stop it, woman! You are crazy, this is ridiculous."

Alex starts the car and drives away at full speed.

"Are you freakin' nuts? Stop this car immediately or I'll have you--"

"What, fired?" She laughs. "On what grounds, huh?"

The car ends up in front of her house, and she unlocks the door. Jack is incensed as he examines her thinking unutterable words. "I will never step foot in your house, that's never gonna happen!" he says, firmly.

"What's the concern? We're two highly intelligent, vibrant and attractive go-getters? We have so much in common," she tells him, feeling defeated. "Just go, go ahead, you can get out now, and you can walk back."

Holding the door open he gives her a few parting words. "No, actually. I have a lot more in common with the woman I have at home. She has common sense, while you're just common with no sense. She's the woman I love and promised to stand by, no matter what. I do hope you find a man that feels that way about you. I really do. Good night."

Walking away he feels a sting across his back. The sound of tin hits the ground. She has thrown a half-empty soda can at him.

Back in his car, emotions from the entire day come full circle at the moment. *What is my wife going through?* One tear leaves his eye and runs down his cheek, flowing into his mouth. Upon returning home, he finds Kelly awake but in bed. She's reading her Bible even though that's usually their morning routine together. He's hoping she doesn't sense how rattled he's feeling.

"Hi, baby. How are you doing?" he asks. "Where's

Tiffy?"

"I sent her home an hour ago. Jack, you've been gone quite a long time, and you, well, you've been quite busy lately, honey."

He bounds toward her, getting in the bed to embrace her as if holding on for dear life. "I love you, Mrs. Kelly Riley. And quite honestly, I wouldn't know what to do without you. How are you feeling, sweetheart? Are you feeling okay? I'm going to take a little leave to spend more quality time with you, okay? We'll work this out, God, you and me."

She looks at him and smiles. "Jack Riley, I love you too, and I only hope I've been the kind of wife you've always wanted."

"Kelly, dear, I've been thinking. How 'bout we make an appointment to see the doctor. Let's see if there's something we can do to get you feeling better."

"Like what?"

"Baby, there's nothing wrong with meds. Yes, we have faith, but God uses meds as well," he asserts.

"We tried several different kinds, but none of them worked well enough where I could tolerate the side effects for long," Kelly explains.

"But that was then. It's a new day. We can try something else just to see what our options are," he says. "Just promise me you'll think about it."

She doesn't respond.

"Okaaay, well, turn off the light and let's get some sleep," he manages to mutter, wanting to end the day as soon as possible. "Good night."

She flips the switch off then turns toward him and whispers, "I'll consider the meds but only if you promise to be honest with me."

"Of course."

"You smell like cheap ugly perfume," she says, her voice soft in the darkened room. "Where were you, tonight?"

Jack is outdone. This has not been a good day for him, or his wife. His pulse is rising; he knows he has no choice but to try to explain his unintended nightmare.

"What did you do, Jack?" she presses as she breathes in deeply to keep from crying.

"Kelly, let me explain. It is definitely not what you think. I need you to believe me. I stopped at Bannigan's and someone from the office came in as I was leaving.

"Someone from the office? Who?"

Jack takes a deep breath. "Ugh, it was…it was Alex."

She turns her head away from him. "I should have known."

"Kelly, nothing happened. I walked her to her car and she tried coming on to me. That's it." *No need in telling her every detail.* "I have no interest in that woman, and I made that very clear to her. I informed her of my love for my God-given wife. You don't have to worry for all my love is for you. I put myself in a bad position unintentionally tonight, and for that I'm sorry. I really wanted to believe I was dealing with a rational and sane human being. That woman needs help."

"Well, you let somebody else help her!" Kelly shouts as she begins to cry.

He embraces his wife and wipes her eyes. "Kelly, I would never hurt you on purpose, ever, please believe that."

"I know it's been hard on you lately, but I really need you to stand with me and for me. Keep your big boy pants on--figuratively and literally. I think you'll do that. Trust has never been an issue between us. You've always made me feel safe."

"I am committed to you. I love you, Kell."

She senses his sincerity. *Notes of Jasmine, lavender and I don't know what else* "but can you please take that awful smelly shirt off. It's making me nauseous. Can't you smell it?"

"Look, Kell..." Removing his shirt and throwing on a tee, "I know we've both had a rough day today and our baby bump is almost here but, hmmm, you know, can we, well you know, right now?" asks Jack. "The doctor said you're good to go."

"No."

"Why not?"

"Because I still feel a little annoyed."

"Well, the Bible says don't go to bed angry and do not withhold from one another."

"Good night, Jack."

He grins. *Okay, there's no harm in asking.*

"Good night Kell, love ya." There is silence in the room. "Kelly, I love you." She still doesn't respond. "Did you hear me?"

She smiles to herself. "We wanted to wait, remember the special dress I showed you?"

"Oh yeah, *whoo hoo.* Do we really have to wait that long? Kelly?"

I'll help him out tomorrow with his personal problem.

As morning comes, he lets his staff know he'll be taking time off to be with his wife during the last months of her pregnancy. He explains that there are a few complications and his presence is needed on the home front at this time.

"Family comes first. I'm sure you all understand, and I know the office is being left in good hands. I'm available on a limited basis, if you need me, of course."

He asks his colleague, Benjamin Branson, to assign Alex to someone else outside of his area--out of his sight. "I'm not asking you to fire her, *though I should,* just please assign her to someone else. Please, just do it! I am not in a good place, right now. I don't need any more distractions."

"Wow Jack, did she get to you, too? Have you been

Alexized?"

Jack's eyes cut him in twenty pieces. "No, I have not been Alexized. And I don't want to hear that again. I've been Kellanized."

"Ugh, hmm, I'm not asking any more questions." Benjamin sighs. "But okay, consider it done man!"

Alexandria is livid upon hearing the news of her ultimate move which she believes will lead to her firing. She is more than angry and decides to speak out against Jack. She tells a select few of her friends, those she knew could not keep a secret.

"He came on to me in his office one evening when I was clearly disheartened and upset. I was having relationship troubles, and I knew he could probably give me some wisdom in that area. But instead, he took advantage of my vulnerability. He was all over me like white on rice."

She began to raise her voice, "I was able to overpower him and I ran out of the office, and now he's trying to get rid of me! I could have had him arrested. The nerve of him thinking his reputation or position can't be touched."

The rumors start to fly just as she planned. Alexandria is more than happy to try to destroy him. "I want doubt about him to get out," she says to herself.

"I knew he wasn't as clean cut as he pretends to be," says one female co-worker.

"And I knew Alex wasn't either," says another

behind her back. "Well, she never pretended to be." They cringe then burst with laughter. "The truth is finally out, so devoted to his wife, what a hot mess!"

The news reaches others in his personal staff who confront him. Without going into specific detail, he explains the confusing evening. "It's the whole truth and nothing but the truth. I didn't use good judgment. I was trying to give her the benefit of the doubt."

"Well, we'll have a talk with the office and speak to Alexandria alone to see where her head is at. We will say no more than we have to," says Robert.

"Well, I've asked Benjamin to place her someplace else."

"We still want to talk to her," Robert tells him.

Carter also finds out and asks Jack if he'd like to talk about it. "I'm here for you, man."

"No, I'm done talking about it. The only earthly person I really needed to explain myself to was my wife."

Alex agreed to speak to Robert and other staff superiors. But on the day of their meeting, it is discovered she has vacated her office. On the night before she had cleared out her belongings, a resignation letter is found on her desk along with a note of apology to Jack. The rumors die quickly after that.

"Wow, I didn't get the satisfaction of telling her she needed to move on in so many words," Robert laments.

There is a way that seemeth right unto a man, but the end thereof are the ways of death. - Proverbs 16:25

CHAPTER 16

KELLY'S NINTH MONTH of pregnancy feels like old times. Jack's presence proves to be a healing balm. His love takes her back to her old happy self as the couple eagerly awaits the arrival of Jack Jr. Both families are relieved.

Though he has previously considered leaving his office permanently, during these last few weeks, he feels it makes more sense. His family should come first. He gives needed direction to his staff as he checks in from time to time. Laughing, he asks them, "Do you all think you can get along without me around?" Just asking."

"Well, please don't make us find out," Benjamin says laughing.

Thanksgiving has arrived, and the entire family is

at Emma's for dinner. After blessing the table and before anyone can pick up their forks, Kelly let's out a serious moan. Everyone looks at her, but she looks at her husband.

"I think my water just broke! You are about to be a daddy."

Family members let out surprised, yet joyful sighs. Emma is nervously excited as she and Jack help Kelly to the car.

"Oh, my! It's time! I'll call everyone with details of the good news," she announces as she gets in the backseat with Kelly. As they get closer to the hospital, Kelly's growing anxious as Emma tries to keep her calm.

She is whisked away for delivery with Jack by her side. She asks that her mother be present, as well. They all say a prayer as she kisses her daughter's forehead. "I love you."

Jack takes his wife's hand as she starts to push and grimaces in pain. Under her doctor's stern but comforting orders, she makes one last strained push and a little boy's head appears before fully coming out. There are smiles throughout the room as Jack kisses his wife with tears in his eyes.

"You did it, my love! I'm so proud of you." He peeks at the baby for a split second then kisses his wife again. "He's gorgeous just like you."

Kelly is in awe of her beautiful and healthy baby boy as it is placed upon her chest. She smiles then kisses his tiny head full of black curly hair. Inhaling deeply into the baby's soft and fuzzy head, Kelly drops back as her breathing becomes erratic.

"It's her heart!" yells the doctor.

A sudden flurry of activity begins as the nurse removes the child from her arms and another tries to escort Jack from the room.

"What, what's happening? I am not leaving!" Jack yells, "Get your hands off of me and help her!"

Emma drops to her knees, sobbing in disbelief as a nurse helps her up. She then is escorted from the room. Kelly is still not breathing. The staff works feverishly on her, trying to resuscitate the young mother. Jack's knees feel as if they will give out at any moment as he tries to stand, stunned and silent against the wall, waiting, praying. *Oh my God, did we not pray enough?* He tries to refocus on his wife.

The doctors and nurses work on her for about 5 minutes, but it feels like an eternity to her husband. Signs of a more normal heartbeat register but fade away again.

"Please, God. Please, bring her back."

A regular continuous heartbeat registers, but it's not strong. Kelly hangs on by a thread. Anxiety hits Jack like a ton of bricks, and he starts to weep.

"Hang in there, Jack. We're moving her to the ICU," the doctor says. "You should go check on your mother-in-law."

As the doctor leads him away, he looks back at his

wife one more time.

Emma and Jack embrace, and her knees give out in his arms. Rubbing his head, "She's still with us. She's in the ICU, now. Please, let's sit down for a bit."

Emma's phone is constantly buzzing, vibrating, but she is too numb to respond. Family members head to the hospital because the hospital staff will not give them any information over the phone. Tiffy, Jessie, and Laurie arrive.

"What is going on? Where's my mother?" hollers Jessie to the maternal nurse. "Is Kelly alright, is the baby okay?"

The nurse is finally given permission to escort them to a private room where Emma and Jack are seated with the doctor. As they see the solemn faces, they know what they are about to hear will not be the news of a joyful birth.

"What happened to my daughter-in-law and my grandchild?" Laurie interrupts before the doctor can open his mouth.

The girls hug their mother as the wailing begins.

"The grandbaby is fine," Emma says with tears sliding down her cheeks. "Kelly, on the other hand, is not doing so well."

Mrs. Riley covers her face as moisture drips down her cheeks. Jack sits mummified, unable to speak. The constant vibration of his cell can be felt in his pocket.

The doctor states that her heart is gravely weak. "We are doing everything in our power to save her."

"I don't believe you. You've been wrong before!" Jack shouts.

"I understand your concern," the doctor says. "We will keep you posted if anything changes. In the meantime, please be prepared to stay with your baby overnight."

Emma and the girls are distressed as the tears continue to flow. Jack asks the doctor if he and the family can be left alone for a bit.

"Of course."

Jack lays his head on the conference table as the girls put their hands upon him. They all pray. Mrs. Riley leaves to call Antonio and Carter. Jack visits his son alone as an overwhelming empty feeling envelopes the new father.

"God, I need some help here. What do I do?"

In his spirit, he hears, "*Keep standing.*"

Emma is prepared to stay at the hospital with him as they take turns checking on Kelly. Escorting his mother, Tiffy, and Jessie as they leave, all are suddenly bombarded with the press who have gotten wind of the misfortune. He can't believe they aren't giving him space at this time. He walks right past them without saying a word.

Laurie asks her son for the millionth time if he needs company for a couple of days and his repeated respond is, "I can't think, right now."

With a thousand thoughts running through his mind, there are suddenly many decisions to make; his life has taken an unexpected turn. *Suppose she doesn't pull through,* he fears.

After finishing a sullen conversation with his father and brother, he shuts in for the night. Jack spends time with his son then sits with Kelly, holding her hand while praying. Emma has fallen asleep on the small couch in the room. *Hospitals are so quiet at times you have nothing but your thoughts.* His thinking being all over the place, he's unable to sleep watching the monitors. Fear and worry bark at his mind like a rabid dog. *Where's my faith?* Peering at his mother-in-law, he's happy she's able to get some rest, though how restful it is, he wonders.

At 5 A.M. the next morning Kelly's nurse comes in to check on her. Jack is asleep on a chair, face forward with his head lying on the bed. The nurse is startled to see Kelly conscious, trying to speak. She awakens Jack and Emma, then lifts the oxygen mask momentarily so all can hear what her heart is struggling to say.

Jack smiles. "Hey, baby. I love you." He embraces her gently, and Emma follows.

"Hi, looovve you," she says, softly. Though, struggling to breathe, she pushes through her next words. "Can-can I see our son?"

Emma turns away so Kelly cannot see her tearing up. The nurse leaves and comes back with the doctor.

"Please, she wants to see the baby," Jack tells them.

"Of course, please bring the baby," the doctor says to the nurse as he takes Kelly's vital signs.

They hand Jack Jr. to Jack, and he places the child on the bed next to Kelly. Smiling, she looks at her husband and mother. He nods. "Yes, God did it because you believed. I'm so proud of you," Jack says as he starts to weep.

Speaking ever so softly and with labored breath, he leans in to listen. "God gave..." She pauses. "He gave you a SSSSammy." She pauses, again. "Please... take care of him, show him, shhhhow him what love is."

Jack gently kisses her lips. She reaches out for her husband's hand and squeezes it with the little strength she has left. Adrenaline rushes through every vein in his body as he feels her grip loosen. Panic sets in as he embraces her lifeless body with all his might as if it would buy more time.

"No! Wait! I have more to say! It's not supposed to happen like this. Why are you leaving me? Why now, for God's sake, why now? We have a son to raise together. We're supposed to grow old together. This is not fair. I need you, baby. I need you!" Choking with emotion, he smooths her hair back then wipes her brow. "Please, come back. Come back to me Kelly, please!"

Emma embraces her daughter's legs because Jack

won't move out of the way. She can't stop crying, but among all the pain and sorrow, there's a flicker of peace that calms her. "You ran your race well, my child. Now, Charles is welcoming you home." She lays her hand on Jack's back to comfort him.

Jack's face being unrecognizable is of no concern to him at the moment. The doctor places a hand on his shoulder. "We are very sorry. We did everything we could," the doctor laments. "You both have my sincere condolences."

Emma finds strength to call home to inform her daughters. All Jessie can understand is "Your sister is gone." As she repeats those words out loud, Tiffy lets out blood-curdling screams. Jessie's body tenses up as she falls across the couch. Laying there in disbelief, she closes her eyes until she can no longer stand the screams. Embracing Tiffy does little to calm her down.

The baby is released to come home with his father. Jack calls his mom with the news, and she's speechless.

"Honey...I'm at a loss for words. I just want to wrap my arms around you and the baby and never let go. I need to see you. I'd like to stay with you and my grandson, tonight."

"Of course. I will need you now more than ever."

The ride home is solemn. Emma is seated in the back with the baby and says a prayer over him. Jack feels nothing but emptiness from the vast hole in his heart. His mind keeps reliving his last look at his wife's beautiful face. The tears begin to flow again as he repeatedly slams his fist against the steering wheel.

"God, I feel so angry. I feel so angry. I feel so angry," he screams. "She was too young. I feel cheated."

Emma places her hand on his shoulder. "Jack, stop the car, pull over to the side. Please, stop."

Jack pulls over. "Ms. Emma, I failed your daughter, I failed her."

"You didn't fail her. In fact, there was no man that could have loved her more than you."

Jack lowers his head and continues to cry.

"Jack, look back here, look at your son," Emma says. "He needs you to be strong for him. We're all in this together, remember that."

At home, Jessie and Tiffy are pouring over their sister's short life. "She knew, she knew, she was trying to tell us in her own way," says Tiffy, cupping her face. "She was telling us to prepare. I didn't know she would leave us. I assumed she was going back into her old self, is all."

"I know, that's exactly what I thought the change was all about too," says Jessie as they embrace. "But you know what, Tiffy? She was happy. She was truly happy. She had a life that she never thought she could have. God blessed her with a beautiful child who is a miracle in itself and with a man that was truly God-sent. He used Jack to bring her out of a hole, and we were so doubtful about it. God sent true love her way, and this love unlocked another world for my sister and for that I am grateful," Jessie says.

"I am too, but you know something else, things like this sure mature you. My little sis was such an inspiration to me." Tiffy sighs. "She really was. I admired her so so much, but I don't think she knew just how much. For that, I feel so bad. I feel just terrible." Tiffy starts to weep again. "I was an awful sister to her." She pauses. "Well, oh my, this has been an overwhelming wakeup call for me. Why do we treat those close to us so poorly, at times? Why do we do that, Jessie? Explain it to me. Why? I am begging you to answer me, why?"

Tiffy can't contain her emotions as she sobs. Jessie hugs her even tighter.

"She knew you loved her," Jessie says. "I'm sure of it."

"That still doesn't answer my question." Tiffy slams the door before Jessie could say any more.

CHAPTER 17

UPON ARRIVING AT HOME with Jack Jr., the baby is settled on the living room sofa. Jack sits with him as Emma warms a bottle. His answering machine is filled with messages of condolences and concern.

There is a message from Pastor Robinson, and he returns that call.

"Pastor Robinson, I'm not going to ask why. I am not going to ask that question!" Jack cries.

"Son, you have no idea the conversation your wife had with her heavenly father. And it's not how or why she left us, but it's how she lived. Think of how she lived. Keep those memories as comfort in the coming days. And the Lord would say to you: *Fear not for I am with you, be not dismayed for I am your God; I will strengthen you, I will help you, I will uphold you with my righteous hand. I comfort those who mourn. To be absent from the body is to be present with the Lord. You will see her, again. Take time to grieve, but I will get you through. Love your son."*

"Thank you, Pastor," Jack mumbles with what was left of his voice.

Wasting no time, he calls his father and talks to him about plans to resign from political office. "I've got some savings to tide me over for the time being. I wanted you to be the first to know, Dad."

"Son, you're in a bad place, right now. I think you're reacting too swiftly. Please, take some time. It's too soon to make a decision on that. I've seen the sacrifices you've made and the hard work you've put in on your political journey. Think about what you're throwing away."

"I've made up my mind," Jack says, firmly.

"Son, let us help you to keep your senses at this time," his father begs. "Your mom and I are on our way over to be with you and the baby."

Without another moment's hesitation, Jack hangs up the phone and calls some of his colleagues and superiors telling them of his intentions to resign, effective immediately. Each call encounters long silences from both parties.

"You lost the love of your life, brother. We all know that you are in a hurting place right now, a real bad hurting place, and man, we can't pretend to imagine how your heart is feeling. But all you need is some time, you need more time away," says Robert Foster. "It's ludicrous to be able to even think you can make a decision like this, right now. You're not in your right mind."

"No, that is where you are mistaken, my friend. I have been thinking on this for quite a while, and I think that now would be the appropriate time to step out. I don't need more time. It's what I want to do, and it's done."

"Jack, there is a lot at stake here. You need to finish what you've started. You need to continue with your forward momentum, that is why you keep being reelected. Things have been slow to change, but there is measured progress, you know that!"

"That is exactly what I plan on doing--finishing what I've started. I've started a family; a child is going to need my time and attention. Can you please find a way to gather my staff this afternoon, I would like to speak to them. I am so sorry, Bob."

A call from Carter comes through on the other line. "Hey, brother. I'm so sorry. I don't know what else to say. How are you doing? How's my nephew? I'm on the way over there with Dad and Mom."

The hugs abound when all arrive. "Know that your family is here for you. I love you, man!" Carter responds.

"Mrs. Sanders, I am so sorry. She was a beautiful young lady in so many ways," says Antonio as Carter nods in agreement.

Carter continues, "Yes, I knew from the very first moment I met her how special she was." Pangs of guilt riddle within him. Jack cuts his eyes at him for a split second.

Laurie hugs her son again as he tries hard to contain his tears. Emma isn't as strong and starts to weep.

"I know, Ms. Emma, I know." Laurie hugs her next. "I'm so sorry, honey. It will be alright. Everything is going to be all right. We are here for you."

They all surround Jack Jr. as Laurie holds him. "He's so beautiful. He's just so beautiful."

"Yes, my grandson is a fine one," says Antonio.

The 6 lbs. 5 oz. bundle of goodness in a sea of sadness brings momentary relief.

"Dad, please have a seat, rest your legs. You shouldn't be standing that long. Why didn't you bring the wheelchair?" Jack looks at his brother. "Carter, what happened?"

"He was stubborn this morning," retorts Carter.

"I have something I want to say. So, can everyone just grab a seat for a sec?" announces Jack. "First, I want to thank everyone in this room for your prayers, love, and support. Jack Jr. and I will certainly need more in the days ahead. Family helps us survive during times like these... Umm, but getting to the point, I need to say I've been contemplating leaving the office ever since I met Kelly." Heavy sighing is heard. "To be honest, political life no longer has a hold on me, and I've been feeling this way for such a long time, now. I think what happened solidified the decision for me, but it didn't start there. Maybe the timing is not right, but I'm just not feeling it, anymore."

Carter is the only one somewhat surprised.

"I am not surprised," Emma replies.

"If that's what you feel is best then I'll leave it alone," his father says.

Carter puts his head down and has nothing to say as Jack looks at him. Carter feels his brother is throwing a dream away without much thought, at all.

"Not exactly understanding my next move, but it will come in time, it will come. I have no doubt about that. My mind is not right at present."

Carter declares, "Now, you're right about that, Jack!"

"Carter, this is not the time," Antonio says.

Jack ignores his comment. "I only know right now my focus is on my son and I'm going to need some help."

The doorbell rings as Tiffy and Jessie arrive. The door opens but they pause momentarily, unsure as to whether they are ready to face reality. Tiffy grabs onto her mother, squeezing her with all the strength she has remaining while Jessie embraces them both. As they behold their beautiful nephew, their pain subsides briefly.

The new dad wants to be alone for a moment with this son. He introduces him to his new home. Carrying him around the room, he remembers the excitement of activity in preparation. The chords of "Tender Love" spew from his mouth softly and tenderly as he gazes at Jack Jr. He lays the baby in his crib as he composes himself. *Jack Grayson Riley,* he reads over his bed and smiles.

"You may all come up now," he tells his family. "I'm leaving for the office to make my announcement. I know baby Jack is in good hands."

"So much activity in one day, Jack?" Tiffy asks.

"Yes, are you sure you need to do this today?" Laurie asks. "Why not give it a couple of days while you think more on it and rest?"

"No, all I can think about is my son, right now. I have to start making arrangements for Kelly's home-going."

"May I and the family please take care of that, Jack?" Emma pleads. "I'll present my plans to you for your approval. I think you will be pleased." Emma smiles and so does he.

"Of course, I would like that, thank you. There's one thing I need to ask of someone. Well, I have..." He rubs his hands across his forehead. "A picture of a dress that Kelly adored. Not sure if you'll be able to find it, but I believe it can be made in time."

"Yes, absolutely," says Jessie. "She will have that dress. My sister will have it." Jessie begins to wail with grief for the first time upon seeing the picture of the dress. The reality has finally hit her.

Jack, his father, and brother leave for the office.

The staff's all gathered, waiting for the announcement. The sense of loss and foreboding saturates the atmosphere. Jack arrives and hugs as many staffers as he can, all expressing their condolences and concerns. Their guy has lost someone special, and they know they are about to lose someone special, as well. As he stands before the crowd and surveys the room, there is complete silence. He lowers his head and then raises it, again.

"Thank you, thank you, thank you for your love and outpouring of kindness to my family and me. You have no idea how wonderful it is to know that people truly care. I've got a new life ahead of me now. For *things* are different now. I thought when I started on this thrilling and humbling ride with you all, that we would all finish together. But that's the *thing* about this ride called life. You will encounter many bumps along the way, some small, some large, and then there are some so big you hold on with all your faith in God, so you don't fall off as you're rocked from side to side. Need I say more?"

It's a rhetorical question. No one answers. "Effective immediately, I am stepping down from my office." There is a gasp, then silence from the audience. "I pray that I have made a difference in these years, fighting for the people of my district."

"You have, Jack. You have, and we love you!" is heard from someone.

"I love you all, too. I am so grateful to have worked with such a fantastic group of people. There is much caring, strength of character, and an outstanding work ethic in this room. I feel so sad that I have let you down. I have let my constituents down."

"No, no, you haven't let us down. We understand completely," shouts one of his aides, Jamison.

"Thank you, thank you so much for understanding. I pray for a smooth transition and a continuation of the vision for the change we long to see. I thank God for the opportunity for however short this season may have been. It was one of my dreams for change, and lastly, I'd like to thank my father, who's here, who inspired the dream, and I hope I have made him proud."

The two smile at each other and hug.

"Thank you. Peace and blessings to all. Love you guys."

The clapping and hugging begin as Jack sees his way out.

CHAPTER 18

J ACK RETURNS HOME for momentary relief as he realizes he will have to face the public the next day. He vows to keep it short and to the point as he did on this day. Jessie and Tiffy ask him how it went at the office, but he's not in the mood for talking. He proceeds upstairs to his baby's room.

Antonio tells the ladies, "I think the realization of what happened just hit him. It's a bit much for two days."

"Yes, don't we know it, don't we know it," says Tiffy, as all nod in agreement.

The baby is asleep as is Emma in Kelly's rocking chair. Jack smiles. He lowers his eyes in momentary reflection. Swaddling Jack Jr. close to his heart, he heads to his own room. Lying in bed with wide-eyed wonder, he stares at the caramel colored miracle. His large hands trace over his face and head, smoothing back his black hair. In exhaustion, he takes hold of Jack Jr.'s tiny hand and closes his eyes. He's very tired as he sleeps for about an hour. He awakens startled and immediately looks for his wife, before realizing his dream had betrayed him, mightily. He heads downstairs to join the family.

Laurie is preparing formula for Jack Jr. as the others are sitting at the kitchen table, talking.

Jessie chimes in, "Jack, we've been working on the home-going plans. Have a seat, and we'll tell you what we have so far. We think you'll like it."

"Really, you think I'll like the plans? You want me to sit down and look at funeral plans for my wife?" Jack shouts. "Do you know what I've had to endure in the last two days? And then there's tomorrow and the next day and the next! I've lost the love of my life, I'm quitting my job, I've got a newborn son to raise, I have to speak to the public tomorrow, and my phone won't stop ringing!"

"Jack, stop it!" cries Laurie.

Raising his hand in demonstration, "I've had it up to here and down to there. So no, I don't want to hear discussions on funeral plans and I don't want to make any more freaking decisions, right now. You got that, huh, you got that?" He walks out of the room.

"Please forgive my son," pleads Antonio. "I've never

seen him act that way."

"We already have. We understand even more now. We have all suffered a deep loss, but he is hurting on so many different levels," Emma states.

They all prepare to leave except his mother. Antonio approaches Jack to see if he's alright.

"I'm okay. I apologize for my stupid behavior."

"It's alright, we all understand," says Antonio. "We're all leaving, now. Get some rest if you can."

As Emma is tending to Jack Jr. before leaving, Jack walks in and offers a sincere apology.

With a half-smile and compassion in her eyes, "Son, we understand the pressure you are under. Jessie is alright. We know what you said was out of hurt and frustration, putting on that grand display," she says.

They both smile.

"A grand display, huh, is that what it looked like?" He laughs.

"It was the grandest I've ever seen from you. You know, I'm not seeing you continuing in politics either, you should take up acting!" she says with glee. They both have a chuckle, again.

"It's nice to find something to laugh about, right now. Laughter is indeed good for the soul, real medicine for a broken spirit," says Emma while grinning at Jack Jr.

"Yes ma'am, it sure is."

"Well, this is my one and only grandbaby, our miracle child, and I pray it's not the only one I'll ever have. Kelly was a pioneer in so many ways. My two other daughters will get there one day. I've held them too close. I should have pushed them out a long time ago," says Emma, amusingly.

Laugher again permeates the atmosphere.

"Mrs. Emma, there's somebody for everybody, and I can almost guarantee that Tiffy will surely give you another grandchild," muses Jack.

"Well, she better do it the right way," Emma says. "I mean, after *the one* finds her." She burps the baby and hands him to his father. "He's ready for bed now. I'll let you have the honors."

"Mrs. Emma, I've been thinking back through the years, the circumstances, the experiences, the fears, the triumphs. Yes, we went through it all, and now there has been a hesitation of this life on earth, and we all have to pass that way, but sometimes you just want to know why. She was so young. I told Pastor Robinson I wasn't going to ask that question but who doesn't ask? Who really doesn't want to know in the deep recesses of their heart?"

"Yes, son. Yes, indeed," Emma says, wiping her eyes. "We won't know 'till we get to the other side. You know something... I keep seeing you in the pulpit. I keep getting these visions."

Nodding his head in acknowledgment, "You never know, you just never know."

Emma and her daughters return home. Their mother shuts herself off in her bedroom. The night brings unusual silence and calm into the house. For the first time in her life, Tiffy's mouth is silenced. The ladies check in on their mother as Emma has prayed for rest.

Knocking on her bedroom door, "Mom, how are you doing?" asks Jessie.

"I'm okay. I just want to be alone." She is deeply disturbed but knows her daughter is in a good place--free of all confusion and pain. *I will see my daughter again so help me to rest in you Father, for you comfort those who mourn.*

The ladies peer into their sister's old room, pause for a second then close the door.

Jack's in bed contemplating his speech for the following day. An uneasy feeling permeates his mind and body. He reminds himself to make the speech short and sweet. Perhaps, the shortest he has ever made in his life. Suddenly doubts--serious doubts--start to overtake his mind regarding leaving his office.

A lifelong dream has come about, and I'm about to throw it all away. Would Kelly have wanted me to do this? Is it really best to step down? Surely God will help me with my son. Did I make a decision too soon out of fear and frustration? Surely, there's more for me to accomplish before leaving.

God, please show me a sign. Am I doing the right thing? Should I have not been so quick with my prior decision? I am so confused. It was probably a rash decision, as all have said to me.

He felt compelled to go into his son's room. The night light is softly illuminating his son's cherubic face as he hears in his spirit, *"Finish what you started, son. Finish what you started for your son. Finish just for now, but I am calling you higher in me though your time is not yet. I have put a word in your mouth. Remember asking me to lead and guide you but you have not consulted me again. I am here. Go forth for I am with you."*

He knew at that moment it would all work out. He breathes a sigh of relief as the uneasiness leaves his mind. That half of the load has been lifted from his shoulders, but the other half is the deep ache for his wife. He has a son who will never know his mother. He is embarrassed to make this next phone call, but he knows he must, right away. He calls Robert and tells him of his plans to stay on the job. There is a long pause on the other end of the line, then laughter from both parties.

"Jack, I'm sure glad you came to your senses and made the right decision. Your timing is terrible, man! You have certainly put me in a spot, but it'll be alright, it'll be alright man. For you Jack, I'm on it."

"I know Rob, and I sincerely apologize for having to put you through this. It seems that's all I've been doing lately is apologizing. Please make the calls for me, and I'll be forever indebted to you. Thanks for standing by me," pleads Jack.

As his decision has been reversed, he decides to hold a press conference instead of facing the public.

As he speaks to reporters, "I have suffered a tremendous loss, but I've gained a tremendous blessing with my son. What has taken place in my life over the last couple of days almost stopped me from finishing my course. I will continue for now. We will work a little longer and harder to continuously move forward." He answers only a few questions then gets ready to leave. "My other life--my son--is calling me, right now. Thank you."

So when this corruptible shall have put on incorruption, and this mortal shall have put on immortality, then shall be brought to pass the saying that is written, Death is swallowed up in victory. O death, where is thy sting? O grave, where is thy victory?
- 1 Corinthians 15:54-55

CHAPTER 19

At HOME, JACK FINDS that Laurie has left for the day to tend to Antonio while Tiffy is watching his son for the night.

"Tiffy, I really wanna thank you guys for helping me through these first nights. There's so much I have to focus on. Thank You."

"Jack, we're going through it as well, and nothing could make us happier right now than to spend time with this baby. So, you take the time you need. We are all here for you." She then asks about the press conference.

"It went as well as could be expected. I am staying on a little longer."

She gasps as he quickly changes the subject.

Holding his son, he is now interested in hearing of the home going details. Tiffy spares no details and lets him know the special dress is being worked on, as they speak. "As we said before, she will have it."

They both smile.

"Thank you, the home going will be special," he says. "Okay, now give me some more tips for my main man. I've got to take good care of him so his mama will be proud. Tomorrow, I would like it to be just him and me. My day is cleared only for him, but you guys have been most wonderful in everything. I know you're hurting, too."

Tiffy softly speaks almost in a whisper. "Yeah, I miss my sweet little trailblazer so much."

"I know you do."

She pauses, momentarily adrift in thought and reflection. She tightens her jaws to keep back the tears in front of Jack. She clears her throat. "So, uh, I'm sure you've heard a million times already but the baby should sleep on his back. Also, you won't look good with bags under your eyes, but you'll get used to it. Do you have any plans for a nanny? I'm sure my mother would love to look after him."

"Yeah, now that might be a little tricky; my mama wants the baby, too!"

They both laugh.

"They would need to learn to share, that's all. Now back to the sleep loss and bags, seriously you went there?"

"Yup, comes with the territory!"

He laughs.

They both depart for the night. Tiffy sleeps in the spare room, next to baby Jack's room. Jack puts the baby to bed as he reclines next to him in Kelly's special chair. He is too tired to find the missing cushions. Though the chair is uncomfortable, the sleep comes fast.

Almost immediately, the loud and piercing cry of baby Jack awakens Jack and Tiffy. She is unaware Jack is in the child's room already, consoling Jack Jr. As she reaches the doorway, he turns and looks toward her. His gaze is fixed much longer than it should. She begins to feel uneasy. Unbeknown to her, Jack's envisioning Kelly in his mind. He longed for his wife to be standing at that door, beholding him and their child.

Thinking what she should not, Tiffy glides over to him gazing longingly as she touches his arm. He doesn't move as he's in a momentary trance. She moves her face closer to his as she inches toward his lips. Before they touch, reality sinks in. He recoils quickly in astonishment.

"Uh, uh, oh my, hmmm, I, I am sorry, I am so sorry, please forgive me. My mind has been crazy these last couple of days. I don't know what I was thinking or doing." Tiffy starts to weep. "I didn't mean for that to happen."

"It's alright. It's alright. I'm sorry, as well. I think

we're all a little spacey, right now. Please, I've got this. You can leave now. You should probably head on out first thing in the morning."

As the sun arises, Tiffy is preparing to go home. Emma calls with the news that she, Jessie, and Mrs. Riley will be taking turns as long as Jack needs them.

"Tiffany Shirlene Sanders, you don't need to be there," Emma says.

"I know, Momma. How did you know? I feel so ashamed!" Tiffy cries.

"I sensed it in my spirit, daughter. I should have known better. You being there alone is certainly not a good idea. He's vulnerable right about now. Come on home and get in your prayer closet!"

"Mom, Jack wants to be alone with his son today. I'm on my way home," Tiffy says.

"Well, come on child!" Emma says.

"Mom, I don't mean to act like that. I don't want to be that way. What's wrong with me?"

"It's called renewing the mind, Tiffany. God's got a good man for you when you're ready."

Alone time attending to his son is proving to be a very pleasurable experience for the new father. He is enjoying being a caretaker to someone so precious and vulnerable that needs him. "See, Jack Jr., see what your momma did in love for you? See your awesome room, your teddies, your little buddies on the wall?"

His face turns sour as a melancholy moment briefly interrupts. "Hey man, let's go get something to eat. It's only me and you," Jack tells the baby. "How about a chili dog and a milkshake? Can you handle a milkshake, little man? Siiikee, fooled ya!"

Mrs. Riley calls. "I'm on my way to check on you and spend some more quality time with my grandson. I know I haven't been able to stop by more due to your father's ailments, but Carter will sit with him today."

I really don't want any company today but how can I refuse? "Okay, Mom. What time are you coming?"

Emma calls him right after. "Jack, I'm calling to check up on you and my grandbaby. Are you alright? Do you need any help, today?"

"No, I'm doing pretty well, Mrs. Emma. My son and I are about to relax with some chili dogs washed down with milkshakes and then take in a movie."

"Don't you even try that with me now," she tells him. "By the way, the dress is ready for Kelly, and it's absolutely beautiful, just as my baby was."

"Great, I, uh, I guess that's good. I would like to see it tomorrow. What time will you be stopping by?" asks Jack.

"Late afternoon."

"Okay, see you then. Thank you, Mrs. Emma."

"You don't have to thank me, son. That was my

child--my special child--for the short time that I had her. Thank you, Lord. I did my best. Jack, you have your son, love your son. I'm so grateful to God that he gave you and me something through her to continue to love, a reflection of Kelly, so very grateful!"

"Mrs. Emma, you are reflecting what is in my heart, you've read it. I'll see you tomorrow," he says.

CHAPTER 20

SWADDLING HIS NEWBORN, Jack pauses to reflect on what he would like to share with the world about who his wife was. A good feeding renders Jack Jr. a heavenly sleep, something Jack wishes he could have. He decides to go through his appointments and check his voicemails and inbox, again. This is really the best downtime he's had in a while.

His mother arrives about an hour later and they hug. "Honey, how are you doing?" she asks.

"I am coping, for now. I've got a son to raise, a beautiful son."

"Yes, you do. Where is my baby?"

"He's asleep. He's been fed."

"Okay, I'm going to spend time with him just

sitting."

"That's fine. I need to work on some things, anyway."

In his home office, he pours through his messages and one caller is Alexandria.

"Hi, Jack." Her voice wasn't as vicious as the last time he'd heard her. "I haven't been able to get a hold of you. I'm sure you're busy. Anyway, I merely wanted to say how sorry I am for your loss. I do hope you are okay. If you need to pour out your soul, I'm residing in San Diego at the moment. You can look me up. I think you know how to find—" The answering machine cuts off before her message could finish.

"Take care, Alex," Jack mumbles with half a scowl. "Trust me, I won't be looking for you." Listening to more of his messages he finds there are many from various women he's never heard of. *How did they even get my number?*

"Hi, Mr. Riley. So sorry for you and your child but now that you are single again, uh, I am available if you ever get real lonely," one caller says.

"You have my sympathy," says another unfamiliar voice. "But I'm here if you get lonely—" Jack deletes yet another message and decides to take a break.

Laurie looks into his office. "Hey, baby. What are you doing?"

"Oh, only going through my appointments and voicemails." Jack leans back, rubbing his tired eyes. "Listen, I'm going out for a ride, need to get some air.

Call my cell if you need me."

"Oh, okay." Laurie sounded a bit deflated. "I was hoping we could do a little talking, sweetie?"

"Mom, I need to get away for a few, won't be gone long."

Laurie just smiles. "I'm concerned about you, son. We've hardly talked about what has happened. I need to know how you're really dealing with this. I'm your mother."

"Well, everyone handles grief differently. When I'm ready to talk, I will. Right now, I want to get some air and talk to God. I'm gonna head on over to Medgar Everson Park. It's peaceful to me."

She smiles again. "Well, I did raise you right. See ya in a little bit, son."

"You know, on second thought, there is one thing I want to say to you." Jack stops in front of his mom. "It's something about my past that I want to reveal to you."

Laurie faces him, looking upward at his tall frame. She places her hands on each of his shoulders and stares into his eyes. "Son, I already know what it is. You don't have to tell me anything. I prayed for you back then as I am now. Nothing else needs to be said about that period of your life. That case is closed."

CHAPTER 21

RIDING AROUND HIS BELOVED city of Jackson, Mr. Jack Riley stops at Medgar Everson Park. The serene space is pretty empty for such a nice early fall day. A young woman walks past, pushing a stroller. Jack smiles as he thinks of these future moments with his own son. Breathing in the crisp air, he takes note of the brown and orange tinged leaves falling. *Kelly's favorite season and mine as well.* Though dusk is at hand, he puts on his aviators and a Jackson State baseball cap. Perching on a bench almost overshadowed by trees, he watches passersby. *Seems like a good hideaway.* He's reflecting on his bride.

Spend more time with her? I believe I gave her the best that I could, all I had in me. I'm supposed to know what to do to take care of my family--have all the answers, right? Men don't like failure, but no earthly man has all the answers. I keep learning that over and over again!

Unconsciously, maybe I have been trying to be perfect and everybody's savior. Maybe, that's why I was drawn to her. Maybe my brother was right. Nah, he was most definitely wrong. And perfect, heck, only a few know that I'd dabbled in drugs in my younger years and my temper belies even me sometimes. Wiping his brow, *Hmm, it was only the grace of God that pulled me away from the road of drugs. I always thought it would have broken my mother's heart at the time to have known, but now I know she knew all along. Her choirboy was strung out. She never let on.*

He recalls his college years at Yale. The studious Jack ended up at a party he knew he had no business attending. As he told his father later, his roommate wanted to show him a new way to relax. He knew the danger of drugs and had avoided this kind of interaction many times before, but he didn't want to seem so out of touch and holier than thou this one time. *Just one taste and you'll be hooked, Jack. Just one taste and you'll be hooked,* his mind warned him, but still, he reasoned he was strong and could easily walk away. But he did not leave that night. In fact, he came back many nights. His family could not reach him for days on end, and when he happened to answer his calls, he always had a good excuse--he was deep in study and couldn't be disturbed.

Antonio felt something was not right and asked Carter to make a surprise visit. A revelation of drug abuse left his father and brother highly disappointed, to say the least. Jack and Carter both pleaded with their father not to share the information with Laurie. To her, Jack was her baby who could do no wrong.

His disrespect for the power of the draw had changed. He wanted to be free of his condition at all cost. The push from his family was the forward momentum he needed to proceed with treatment. Carter took a leave from his physician duties to spend time with him during his rehab. It was not an easy journey. At times, Jack didn't know if it was worth the fight, but he kept seeing his mother's face. He did not want to disappoint her.

I realize how I got into that mess, but I sure thank my father and brother for standing by me. Carter telling me he never thought it could happen to me. Well, it could happen to anybody. It was hell for both of us as I was trying to keep up with my studies as well. Whooa. We both can laugh about it now. At one point, Carter wanted to check his own self in. Jack smiles. *Man, I have so much respect for those that can get through this and not go back.*

Jack learned a hard lesson about following his own mind. He was well aware he had to stay on track as to not be drawn back into that lifestyle. His prayer was, *God, I'm giving my life back to you. I'm asking for wisdom and strength to stay the course. Let the sight, smell, and taste ever remind me of what I went through and bring me to my knees. I make a vow to serve you and the people, the remainder of this life.*

Well, so much for the past. God, at the moment I'm just a ball of confusion. What are the next steps? You gotta lead me 'cause I don't want to act on my own.

Two hours have passed as he's sitting at the park. He fails to grasp how quickly time has slipped away. The night is upon him as he makes his way back to his car. Checking his phone, there are many calls but none too important. His mother hasn't called, so he knows the baby's okay. Feeling better and stronger after pouring out his feelings to God, he decides to take one more ride through his city. Hopping on the freeway, he exits at Chalmers Street into a more underserved area. A part of town he knows pretty well.

Passing one liquor store after another sprinkled in between boarded up establishments, he stops in front of 5210. *We've come so far, but yet we have far to go. This is why I have to continue the fight whether in politics or the pulpit.*

Suddenly pop, pop, pop pierces the atmosphere as his heart lands in his throat.

"What the...?"

A bullet has shattered his back passenger window, and another has penetrated the driver's side. He slid down as fast as the bullet that narrowly missed. The screech of tires trail off past him. He stays down, visibly shaken while praying. *The angels are watching over him,* he reasons. Looking up, he notices a small crowd has gathered around his car. A young woman asks if he's alright.

Waving his hand, "I'm okay." He steps out to survey the damage. When he returns to the driver's side, an unknown gentleman steps in front of the door to block him. Jack glares at the fellow as if he could to tear his head off, before his countenance changes and he smiles.

Use wisdom, Jack.

The other person returns a smile. "I was jus' kidding, man. I was jus' kidding," the stranger says as he walks away. "Hey, but don't I know you from somewhere?"

"Yeah, I'm one of the ones fighting for you, brother."

Jack drives away as quickly as he can while trying not to draw too much attention with busted out windows. He will call authorities once he's home--*or will he?* he surmises.

The garage door rises for his battered Mercedes and battered pride as he pulls into the driveway. *No, why should I hide this car?* He changes his mind.

Laurie hears him approaching the house and comes out to greet him. Seeing the car damaged, she covers her heart with her hands, visibly shaking.

"What's going on, what happened, are you alright, where in the world were you?"

He pauses momentarily, trying to gather his composure. A long sigh is heard as if he just remembered he needs to breathe. "Well Ma, you could say I was in the wrong place at the wrong time or in the right place at the wrong time. Depends on how you want to look at it. But I was protected by angels."

He calls Robert and then the authorities. Jack tries to calm his mother as he explains what happened. Robert arrives only minutes before the cops as Laurie returns to the house at Jack's request. The neighbors all gather around when the cops arrive. Mr. Winston, his next door neighbor, inquires if he's okay. Jack tells the cops that he has no idea who it was and that he didn't see anything as he was looking in one direction upon the first shot and his head went down immediately after that.

"I just heard a car pass afterwards. You can ask those that hang out in the immediate vicinity if you can get anything out of them," he says, exasperated.

Jack goes on to explain that he had to leave the scene or he would have been in even more danger.

"Listen, I'm seriously tired. It's been a rough day, and I'd like to wrap this up now. If you have any more questions, I would be happy to answer them in the morning."

"Do you think the offender might have known who you are?" one of the officer's asks.

"Does it really matter who I am? This should not happen to anyone." While rolling his eyes and shaking his head, he goes on. "Lately, this sort of thing is starting to happen more and more in this city, and it's sickening. We need to do something about it. I wanted to help clean up some of the neglect in these neighborhoods. This was my passion, but we've got to get past the dead rail in Congress. The problems in this town are going to take serious action and not just talking heads."

The authorities are satisfied with what they have for the moment. After examining the car, they leave the scene.

"How'd you end up over there?" Robert asks. "It looks like you need security man and..." lowering his voice he adds, "a gun."

Jack waves him off and turns to leave. "Thanks for coming Robert, but you can go now. Good night."

Jack immediately checks on Jack Jr., pulling him against his chest as tightly as he could. *Thank you, God, for sparing my life tonight. Let me be around to raise this young soul with your help.* He asks his mom to stay the night as it is late.

"I'm sure Carter doesn't mind hanging with Dad, tonight," Laurie says. "I will brief them on what happened and tell them you're okay and that you'll talk tomorrow."

Laurie eggs him on to talk more about the events of the night, but he is in no mood to go there, again.

"Okay, son. You've had a rough week. We can talk tomorrow. I am so thankful and full right now."

CHAPTER 22

THE NEXT MORNING, the phone rings incessantly and wakes the household. Laurie asks Jack if she should answer the landline. His cell is full of text messages and unanswered calls, as well.

"No, Mom. I'll take care of it," he says.

He turns off the ringer on his landline to catch a breather as he looks over the calls. He only returns a few. Laurie informs Emma of the prior night's event. Emma is shocked and thankful for the outcome.

Things become a little quieter as the day wears on and he is ever grateful. "They say no man is an island, but right now, I do need my own island," he says to his mom then asks her if she could stay until the evening.

"Of course I can, just gotta check on your father

'cause he's with Carter, you know."

Emma arrives at Jack's home with swollen eyes. Laurie embraces her as both women sit and share coffee. Emma asks Jack if he's okay.

"I'm doing okay, under the circumstances. A little shaken up but my angels were certainly there for me."

"Thank God!" says Emma.

"Yes, my sentiments exactly," adds Laurie with tears in her eyes. "What would I do without my second born?"

Emma lowers her head as Laurie gasps. "Oh my, please forgive me, Emma. Forgive my temporary insanity and insensitivity. I am so sorry. I meant no harm. It's just been a very trying time for all of us," Laurie apologizes.

Jack looks away from both ladies.

"Forgive me, son."

Emma lets her know that she understands as she hands Jack a box containing the dress he requested. "Now, go pick out some beautiful accessories and other items that she needs."

He takes the box to the bedroom, revealing the beautiful creation. His heart is heavy with emotion as he holds it up and wraps his arms around his chest. The flowy fabric is so soft to the touch as he imagines Kelly wearing it before his eyes. He thinks back to the night she presented the picture to him. Going through her closet, he dumps shoes until he finds the black patent leather cut-outs with the strap across the middle. He grabs the pearl earrings and a matching necklace she wore on their wedding day. He lays these items on the bed as he stands back and decides. *Something's missing, something's missing and I know what it is.* He walks into Jack Jr.'s room and grabs the tiny blue baby book revealing the baby's footprint, birth date, weight, length, etc. Fighting back the tears, he heads back downstairs to join the ladies.

He lays the items before Emma before returning upstairs to bring Jack Jr. down. All chatter ceases. Their concentration has been broken. Laurie swaddles her grandson, smiling. Jack asks Emma to have the funeral home place the baby book across Kelly's stomach and have her hands folded across it. Closing his eyes, he wants to appear strong but starts to sniffle.

Holding the book to her heart, Emma is brought to tears. "Yes, of course."

Laurie hugs her son and his mother-in-law.

The rest of the day is spent reminiscing and laughing. Jack brings up his and Kelly's first night together at the Inn.

"I'm going to go change the baby's diaper," Emma excuses herself, not wanting to overhear that conversation.

"You know, I could not consummate my marriage

on that first night. It took--let's say, a minute--but we finally got there." His eyebrows rise. "Our honeymoon was a little on the rough side at first, but things went very very well after the first evening! I call it, Kelly's Secret."

Laurie shakes her head then smiles. Jack smiles brightly at the memory before his countenance drops.

"I miss my wife, so much. This is a big adjustment."

Emma returns from the room and hands Jack Jr. to his father. "I'm leaving now to get to the funeral home," she tells them.

"I thought I could stay longer, but I really need to get home to relieve your brother," says Laurie. "Do you need anything before I leave, honey?"

"No, the baby and I will be fine," he says. "We're bonding. We've got plenty of formula and diapers. And I've got a book, some phone numbers, and a little sense. Oh, by the way, a nanny search starts soon, will you both help?"

"Do you even have to ask?" Laurie says.

"Right," agrees Emma.

Jack sees them out. He puts Jack Jr. to bed then falls asleep himself. He awakens to a crying child about 8:00 p.m. and shrugs, not realizing he had been asleep for so long. *I gotta get used to this.* The baby sucks the bottle nipple as if this is his last meal ever, as his daddy smirks. Jack Jr. falls asleep again but does not stay that way for long.

"What's wrong, buddaman? I fed you. It's not time

213

to eat again. I want you slim and trim." He cuddles him awhile trying to calm him. "You know your mom could have fed you better than I can. I'm trying to be a good substitute. You gotta teach me but go easy on me, okay?"

The baby's eyes close but only to be wide awake once more after an hour. Jack is starting to get a little frustrated and decides to feed him again. After about 15 minutes they are both awake, yet again. His nerves are frazzled by this point as he calls his mom, embarrassed.

"I've tried everything I know. Should I take his temperature?" Jack asks.

"So, you've tried everything? Hmmm, did you check his diaper, is he soaking wet or something else?" asks Laurie.

"I'm a grown college-educated man. Of course, I checked his--" The diaper is sagging from the weight of urine. He had three diapers on the baby, and the padding was so thick he didn't realize the obvious. "Oh, poop."

Laurie is snickering to herself.

"Little Jack, I apologize man. Please be patient with your daddy."

"I think you can take it from here," she muses. "Now, see if you both can get a couple of better hours of sleep."

"Thanks, Ma. I'm just a little flustered, right now."

"That's normal, sweetie. Good night."

Once Jack hangs up with his mother, he lays Jack Jr. on the changing table. "Man, I must really be losing my mind and sense of smell. Okay, we're going to get this right. Your dad is just a little distracted, but I'll get there, partner. I'll get there with you! God, you and me together, little man. We're an unbeatable team!"

CHAPTER 23

VIEWING DAY AT THE FUNERAL home has arrived. Jack has not made up his mind if he wants to be in attendance before the actual ceremony. It is still too painful a thought.

Emma reports back that all is well. "Kelly looks absolutely beautiful, and all his wishes for the day have been arranged. You should come see for yourself. It's my desire that you come on down, Jack. I think it would do you some good."

The sound of sighs and hesitation are all that is heard in Emma's ears. In his mind, the longer he holds out on seeing Kelly, he doesn't have to face up to the fact that she is really gone. For now, he's holding to the premise that she is only away for a short while--

and in all actuality she is. This is his way of coping.

"No, Miss Emma. I won't be there today. I only want one viewing, please. I am grateful for you, so very grateful. I know how very hard this is on you and the girls. I'm sorry."

"Okay son, it's your call. By the way, who will keep the baby while we're at the service?" Emma asks.

"Carter's girlfriend, Lilly. They are stopping by today to see Jack Jr."

Carter and Lilly arrive, and Lilly's bond with the baby is immediate. Cuddling him, she rocks him back and forth. *I really want to do this motherhood thing.* The gaze at Carter is intense as her maternal instinct takes over. His killer eyes have a way of talking back to her which leaves her saddened.

"Lilly, we've had this conversation one too many times," Carter says, trying to soften the blow. "How about we just enjoy watching my little nephew grow up, for now?"

Lilly smiles as Jack catches on and smirks.

"Come on, Lilly. Let me take you on a tour of the baby's room." As they walk side by side, Jack leans in and says softly, "Give him some time, he wants to do this thing right the next time."

Chatting goes on for about an hour while Lilly holds the precious cargo. She returns Jack Jr. to his room as they prepare to leave. On their way out, some of Jack's colleagues drop by.

"We're not staying long, only wanted you to know that we're here for you. We've got your back." Ralph Morse and Tim Goodman pull Jack into a quick hug then tap him on the back. "We'll cover you for as long as you need us, within reason now, brother!"

They all laugh.

"And answer your phone!" Ralph complains. "You and Jack Jr. are not alone."

"I realize that, and your outpouring of concern has been very humbling and sustaining. Trust me, I appreciate it," Jack says. "I need a little time alone to get some sort of balance and get a little stronger in my faith walk, right now."

"If it's okay, can we please get a little peek at the new prince of the house?" asks Tim.

"Follow me, fellas. He's doing what he does best, sleeping and... well, he ain't like me at all. He's a work in progress."

They all snicker.

"He's a fine young man, yes indeed," says Ralph.

"I'm sure there are great things to follow for this one, if he's anything like this father," says Tim.

Jack thanks them for stopping by as they head toward the door.

CHAPTER 24

THE MORNING OF the home-going has arrived and the sun is brightly shining. It pours through the window and reflects upon the baby's face. Jack had placed him in bed next to him the prior night. *His cherubic face looks so peaceful, so sweet.* He says a prayer as he ponders the day's events. He wants to arrive at the service an hour beforehand, by himself. He has asked the limo to pick up Emma and the sisters at their home as he will drive himself.

"Well baby boy, I'm about to be with your momma for the last time on this earth. Oh, we will both get a chance to see her again. I so wish you two could have spent some time together as she wanted you, so very badly, my miracle boy. I, I am so happy she had the vision and God granted her request. I think your momma knew she was leaving this earthly body and you are our connection. She taught me so much, young man."

After a feeding and burping session, he lays him in the crib. "Are you going to be alright little man, while I shower and dress?"

The baby's eyes focus on him as if to say, "Yes daddy, we're a team now."

Leaning over the crib, Jack grins.

After dressing, he spends time on the phone talking to family and friends. Carter arrives to drop off Lilly, and she is more than zealous to hold glances with the baby. Jack heads to the church.

Upon being directed into the chapel room, he hesitates momentarily and sits in the back, looking pensively at the beautiful yellow gold colored casket.

Don't ever lose the kid in you. You're a dream come true for any woman. I want a child of my own. He will be a boy, you got to believe with me.

The memories flood his mind like a raging sea, the good and the uncertainties. Approaching the casket, he musters the courage to behold his beloved. Gazing at her lifeless flesh, he understands it is no longer her—to be absent from the body is to be present with the Lord--for her spirit has moved on. She looks beautiful, as beautiful as the day they met. Her hands envelope the baby book lying across her stomach. She looks so natural. He envisions her waking to chat once more about believing for another miracle. This time, for herself.

"I miss you, baby girl. I miss you so much. I thank God and you for our beautiful son. He's going to make us so proud. I love you, Kelly Riley. So, please ask God to save a good spot for me and our son, okay? Tell Charles I hope to meet him one day as I said before."

Being so caught up emotionally, he's unaware Emma is watching him. She puts her arms around him and they embrace. Other family members soon follow, and the chapel is overflowing with friends and family at the private ceremony.

He feels strong enough to take to the pulpit for reflections. He wants the world to know how special his wife was. "Thank you, God, Pastor Robinson, and to everyone here, I say thank you." He starts as he speaks slowly and methodically. "A mother will miss her daughter. Two sisters will miss their sibling. A son will miss his mother, and a husband will miss his wife. And then there are other family and friends that will miss this angel, as well." He pauses and grabs at his tie. "My wife had a short life that was rather unusual at times. But, she had a good life despite what some believed. In hindsight, I now know why I was drawn to Kelly Denise Sanders on that glorious summer day. It was definitely something beyond that angelic face. It's called a beautiful spirit. Yes, she had a slight handicap, but don't we all. She accomplished everything she wanted in this earthly life. You may not think her life was significant or stood out, but it did. Oh indeed, it did to me." He pauses again, lowering his head.

"Take your time, brother. Take your time," is heard from Pastor Robinson.

"Not everyone is called to a public life or to travel the world or to even work outside of the home, but we are to bloom where we're planted. We all leave our marks in different ways." He twitches his legs trying to release the numbness as he wipes his eyes. "Well, she transferred her beauty mark to our son and me. She wanted to make a difference and feel that she mattered. She beat the odds in every way possible—almost dying upon birth, finishing school, marrying the man of her dreams—yes to her, I was the man of her dreams, can you believe that?" He laughs. "And she gave birth to our miracle son. When she was told she could do none of these things, she came to me and told me that God said *yes*."

"Yeeaaahh," cries Emma, falling into Jessie's arms.

"She told me to never to lose my song and the little child in me and I won't. Kelly was a good wife, and if you ask I will tell you, as the title of the song goes, *She Used to be My Girl*."

The audience smiles.

"She never had a bad word to say about anyone, not even Tiffy." He looks her way and smiles. She cracks a smile through her swollen red face. "And to know her was to truly love her, which is a tribute to that woman sitting right there on the front row, her lovely mother. Kelly's heart and mind were so, *so* innocent. I wonder how in the world she...stood by me! I understand she was in my life to teach me, to truly be my helpmeet, to strengthen my faith and she is why my son is here today. She humbled me. I needed that. And so I want to say to you all that everybody is somebody."

Encouraging murmurs are heard all around the room.

"That's right! Everybody is somebody. And she reinforced my belief in this and in God to continue the fight for others, to continue to lift up those who feel they have no value and feel left out. No one has naming rights over God's children except God, so let no man label you. You may have visible scars. You may have started out at the bottom or fell back to the bottom and feel like you can't rise again, but that's okay. As God told my wife, he's telling you too: *Yes, you can.*"

All faces in the audience are smiling.

"So, I say to you," Jack concludes. "Never, ever give up. Kelly said she wanted to be remembered as accomplished, an overcomer and someone in a sea of people that mattered. Well, I hope I have done her good with my words today. And as an even bigger tribute, I am going to start a foundation for *special children* in her memory."

"Hallelujah!" is heard from the audience as Emma

breaks down, again. Laurie reaches over to console her.

"Sometimes we don't get all of the answers we desire on this side of life but as the scripture says, *And we know that all things work together for good to them that love God, to them who are the called according to his purpose."*

"Ahem, ahem," is heard as he clears his throat.

"Thank you for being here today and listening to our story. Each of you has been a part of our life's journey. Please, look to him who is faithful even in despair for strength. I may have been knocked down, but I'll get back up. Whenever you're ready for me to take that other call, God, I will be ready. Thank you!"

After the service is over. "Hello, I'm Benjamin Walker. I'm the new Deacon at Hill Valley. What's your name?"

Tiffy is caught off guard. "Ugh, hi I'm, I'm Tiffany Sanders."

"Nice to meet you. I merely wanted to offer you my sincerest condolences. I lost my younger brother, let's see, it's been about six months now. So, seriously, if you ever need to talk it out and need a listening ear, I'm certainly available."

Wow, God is it my turn now? I can't even think about that right now...but I'm open!

Jack slowly walks out of the service to the chords of *Tears of a Clown*, one of Kelly's favorites, playing in his mind.

THE END

"For God so loved the world, that he gave his only begotten Son, that whosoever believeth in him should not perish, but have everlasting life." - *John 3:16 King James Version (KJV)*

ABOUT THE AUTHOR

As a first time novelist, Theresa Laws resides in the Chicagoland area. A lover of all things creative, she is also a published songwriter and looks forward to finishing her collection of new works in book and song. She likes to read and write as she is inspired. An accomplished flautist and sewing skills can be found in her repertoire as well.

51012985R00130

Made in the USA
Middletown, DE
29 June 2019